WOLF DENIED

ENSNARED BY THE PACK: BOOK 2

TESSA COLE

Gryphon's Gate Publishing

Wolf Denied

Copyright © 2022 Tessa Cole

Gryphon's Gate Publishing
550 King St. N.
PO Box 42088 Conestoga
Waterloo, ON
N2L 6K5

Print ISBN: 978-1-990587-06-1

AUDREY

THE PLAN WAS SIMPLE. WALK INTO A LAND WHERE A DEATH god slept, go to his altar, and cast a spell to kill my unwanted mating bond with Knox.

Except from everyone's expressions, I doubted it was as simple as it sounded.

There were probably monsters between here and there, like those grimalkins that had attacked the town or worse. But since I'd only been in this realm a few days, I had no idea what to expect or what to fear.

A part of me believed that I should just fear everything. That would be safest. I didn't know anything about where I was or even who I was with... especially the three brothers leading this pack.

Cyrus was enormous and while gorgeous, was gorgeous in a hardened-warrior-dangerous-bad-boy kind of way. If our shifter abilities didn't heal us when we shifted — and if we were in my realm, the mortal realm

— he'd probably be covered in tattoos, wearing a leather jacket, and riding a big, chunky, loud motorcycle. He'd probably throw me to those grimalkins without a hint of remorse if he thought it would protect his pack and wouldn't hurt Knox.

Bishop on the other hand was dangerous in the completely opposite way. Also gorgeous, he had a warm, disarming smile, and was kind, gentle, and supportive, and while I didn't think he'd purposely hurt me, he could easily break my heart. He'd probably left a trail of broken hearts all over town and didn't even know it.

While Knox... Knox hated me. Even if binding my soul to his had been an accident — and I wasn't sure he completely believed that — I'd still trapped him in a mating bond, and I could feel his hatred for the bond and me with frozen certainty in the core of my being.

And just thinking about it made the cold hollowness surge, swirling in and around the aching, desperate need to seal our mating bond with sex.

But the desire to have sex with him — or hell, one of his brothers — wasn't the real emotion in all of that. It was his rejection of me and I couldn't blame him. My power was so low I wasn't worthy to be anyone's mate let alone the mate of someone powerful enough he could be the alpha of his own pack... if he had any desire to lead.

On top of that, I couldn't even shift. My wolf was still asleep. It hadn't woken on the summer solstice of my eighteenth birthday like it should have nor after four more awakening ceremonies, and I feared the wolf half of my soul would never wake. I feared I never had a wolf form in the first place and everyone was mistaken about me being a shifter.

Sure, my essence said I was a shifter, but how could I call myself one when I couldn't shift?

And who would want to mate with someone like that?

"All right," Cyrus said, his intense, moss green gaze jumping from Knox, still in his enormous black wolf form, to Bishop who sat beside me, his hand resting on my knee in an attempt to steady my soul even though we weren't mates or even close friends. "Deacon, Nova, and Finn can handle leadership and security for the town while we're away. Lucius can take over when he gets back."

Bishop nodded his agreement, but Whil, the stunning fae with an ever-so-slightly perpetual golden glow, frowned and opened her mouth to say something.

"I know it isn't wise for the three of us to walk into a death god's realm," Cyrus said before she could argue with him. "But until I'm dead, I'm still the alpha of this pack. It's my decision."

Whil's bright green eyes narrowed. "You'll have to inform Nova that if things go badly, she and Deacon will need to take over."

"Velora is going to love that," Bishop groaned.

The muscles in Cyrus's jaw flexed. "Nova is more powerful and Deacon works better with her."

"You mean Velora is strung so tight Deacon will spend his time riling her up and nothing will get done,"

Whil huffed, tucking a strand of shimmering golden hair behind her delicately pointed ear. Then she turned her attention back to the book that hopefully had the answer to freeing me and Knox from our bond without either of us dying.

"Bishop," Cyrus said as he stood. "Find out everything we need to know about the spell. I'll organize our betas. We'll head out first thing tomorrow morning."

"Tomorrow morning?" I asked, the words jumping out before I could stop myself. "It's morning right now."

I wasn't really a part of this conversation and shouldn't have said anything. Sure, I had to go in order to break my mating bond with Knox, but they hadn't asked my opinion and even if they had, I wouldn't have had one. Hell, I hadn't even heard a quarter of the conversation about breaking the bond because Knox hadn't included me in his telepathic communication with the others.

But waiting until tomorrow meant I had to suffer a whole extra day with the nerve-wracking frozen hollowness of Knox rejecting our bond and the achy longing to have sex to seal it. A longing that was growing stronger and stronger and wasn't focused solely on Knox. My body didn't seem to care who I had sex with as long as I had sex.

And Bishop was just so kind and gorgeous and it was a struggle just sitting in Whil's greenhouse library with him beside me, the heat of his hand burning my flesh through my pant leg.

"It'll take half a day to pack our supplies and organize everything," Bishop said, squeezing my knee, his tightening grip ratcheting up my need and not calming me like he probably hoped.

"And it will take most of a day to get to the closest patrol shed," Cyrus added. "There might be more grimalkins in the area and if we have access to shelter, we shouldn't ignore it. Whil, have you got a map of the area?"

"Somewhere. Give me a minute to find it," she replied.

"You've got until tomorrow morning." Cyrus turned and headed toward the door of Whil's strange greenhouse-English cottage-library as Deacon pushed through the foliage and flowers and hurried into sight.

"The hunt team has returned from Darkweald," he said as he picked his way across the uneven floor to get to us in the mismatched seating area at the back. He wore the same black kilt-like-piece of clothing he had at dinner the other night and nothing else, exposing his broad muscular chest and making my desire spike because hey, he was a good-looking guy and my body wanted sex sex sex. He still also radiated the same sense of feralness, but it didn't seem quite as dangerous after watching him roar with laughter at Cyrus's — and my — embarrassment.

His golden-brown gaze jumped over the group of us, hesitating on Knox, and finally stopping on me, and he raised an eyebrow, his lips quirking as if he'd thought of a joke he didn't want to share.

"No sign of the malicious god," he reported, not commenting on what he obviously wanted to comment on — which was me being a part of some conversation between Whil and the three brothers. "But there's magic present in the ruins. Whil should check it out."

Cyrus's expression darkened. "Just great. Okay, change of plans."

AUDREY

"The ruins are on our way," Cyrus said. "We'll go with Whil and Deacon and a small hunt team to check out this magic then head north. Deacon and the team should be enough to protect Whil on the way home."

Deacon frowned. "North of Darkweald? Why are you going there?" His attention jumped to me, his expression strange. Everyone thought because I'd been found in Darkweald Forest, that I'd come from the north somewhere. "Are you going home?"

"I don't think I can go home." And if I could, I wasn't sure I wanted to.

Back home I was the weak, pathetic shifter who couldn't shift and had no status in my pack. The alpha's son — who was now the pack alpha since he'd murdered his father — and his best friend had tried to sacrifice me to a monster for power because they thought that was all I was good for.

I'd only spent a few days here, but I fit in more and was accepted more in this strange realm than I ever did at home. Although I supposed these people could turn on me since I'd already proven I was a terrible judge of char-acter. For all I knew, the moment my bond with Knox was severed Cyrus and Bishop would decide I was worthless, and I'd be back to being an alpha's slave.

"You don't know you can't return home," Bishop said, his tone soft, sending a shiver of need rushing through me.

Deacon's eyes widened and his nostrils flared, while Cyrus's glower deepened, and Knox started to growl.

Swell. I'd just given everyone a big nose-full of my desire because shifters could smell every damn thing and I had no control over my body right now.

"If you're smart, you should wait until her heat is done," Deacon said, his lips quirking again as if he was trying not to laugh. "Or help her get it out of her system."

Yes, please! With Knox... or Bishop... Cyrus would do...

No damn it. Just no.

My cheeks burned with embarrassment even as heat pooled between my thighs.

Jeez. I only thought having sex with them was a good idea because of the mating bond. Knox would never have sex with me, Cyrus was barely being nice to me, and I didn't know if Bishop was only being nice because of his brother.

Did I really want to have sex for the first time with

someone who didn't love me? Hell, who didn't even like me?

Fuck off, Deacon, Knox snarled, his power rolling off him in waves that made me want to slip off the chair and kneel before him in submission. *We leave at dawn.*

With a low, dangerous growl at Deacon that made the man raise his hands in defense and take a big step back, Knox stalked out of the greenhouse.

"You should probably assemble an all-female hunt team," Cyrus added, his voice gruff, and he, too, strode out of the greenhouse with Deacon at his side.

"Please tell me there's a way to control this," I groaned, turning to Whil. Maybe magic would help me get through the next nine or so days it took to get to the death god's altar.

"I wish there was," she replied, "but nothing can affect a mating bond... although I'm surprised at how strong the need to seal your bond is. It's only a few days old. You should have been able to go at least a week or two before your need to seal the bond is too strong to resist."

"Is she also in heat?" Bishop asked. "Would that affect her?"

"Possibly. A mating bond can set off a heat. Nova would probably be able to check your hormones to confirm, but there isn't much she can do about that, either," Whil said, focusing on me. "From what I know about wolf heats, you just have to get through it. Ideally with a partner, or a couple of partners, with decent stamina."

Swell. I bet Bishop had decent stamina. Cyrus too. And Knox... well, he *was* their brother. Stamina probably ran in the family.

Oh. My. God! Stop thinking about sex!

Except— "Heats aren't this powerful in my realm. They increase a woman's sexual desire, but not to the point of driving her crazy."

I'd never heard of a shifter being desperate to have sex with anyone and everyone. Not even one from my pack where our wolf nature and all its instincts burst fully to life when we were eighteen and sometimes overwhelmed us. Not to mention, I still didn't have a wolf form.

"How am I even in heat? I can't shift?" I groaned, frustrated and angry that even though I'd escaped Sterling and Royce and my pack, I was still a slave. Only this time I was a slave to my body's needs.

"Interesting," Whil said as she stood and headed to a bookcase. "There must be something about this realm that affects a female's hormones compared to your realm because heats in this realm are quite strong."

"So more magic?" Just like the magic that let me understand what everyone was saying even though no one spoke English. Except this magic was far more inconvenient.

"I'm sorry," Bishop said, rubbing circles on my knee and turning me on more. "I wish we could wait for your heat to be over, but the longer we wait, the harder it will be to resist the mating bond."

I fought a churning mix of desire and fear. I wanted to break the bond as soon as possible, but I was about to spend nine days — longer if things didn't go well — with two incredibly hot men, and a man my soul said was my mate. I didn't know if I'd be able to hold out against the growing pressure.

"Once this is over you'll be able to choose who you want to spend your future heats with without fear of completing a mating bond," Bishop added.

Yes, with you.

No, damn it.

I stood and jerked away from him, praying a little distance between us would help me. "I'm not ready for this."

"It's okay," Bishop said, his voice soft. "I'll help you."

"With *everything*?" I asked, heat flooding my core and embarrassment burning my cheeks.

"Yes, even with sex, if that's what you want. No expectations."

Oh God, yes.

Except a small part of me, the part that wasn't desperate and needy or grieving from Knox's rejection said having sex with Bishop was a terrible idea.

"I don't know. I'm not— I haven't—"

I'd only ever had sex in my dreams and only recently at that. Not to mention, I knew the real thing would be nothing like what I'd fantasized about. Hell, I hadn't even really kissed a man since my first kiss with Royce didn't count.

Sex also meant complications. If we couldn't break the mating bond, Knox and I were going to have to figure out our relationship and my original reasons for not having sex with Bishop were still the same. I didn't want Knox angry because I'd slept with his brother. That would be bad for me, but also bad for Bishop and his relationship with his brother.

Wolves were notorious for being possessive and it wouldn't matter if I'd had sex with Bishop while Knox and I were trying to break the bond. He could still end up furious.

Except not everything in this realm was the same as my realm. Maybe wolves here weren't possessive. Maybe Knox wouldn't care.

My need tightened into a desperate ache and my breath picked up. Bishop was kind and gorgeous. Maybe it wouldn't be so terrible for him to be my first even if neither of us wanted a relationship. Women had casual sex all the time.

Except any kind of sex came with the risk of pregnancy and I wasn't on birth control. Merrick, my pack alpha — my *old pack* alpha — and the man who'd raised me after my father had died, wouldn't have ever bothered with the expense and there'd been no one in the pack I'd wanted to have sex with so it hadn't been worth the humiliation to ask for it.

I'd just have to hold myself together.

And if I couldn't?

Fuck. I didn't know if I could.

"Please tell me you have birth control in this realm," I groaned.

"Neva can set you up," Bishop said, standing and gesturing to the door. "Her main office and clinic are in the north wing."

"I think she's still at the hospital helping with the injured from the grimalkin attack," Whil said absent-mindedly, pulling a book from her shelf.

"I'll come back to learn about this spell and help you look for that map." He turned his warm brown gaze to me and my pulse stuttered. "Remember," he said his voice soft and low. "You don't have to be afraid and you don't have to deal with this alone."

Except if I didn't want to break down and jump him or Cyrus, being alone would probably be best.

AUDREY

BISHOP LED ME OUT OF WHIL'S STRANGE ENGLISH COTTAGE greenhouse and my gaze instantly jumped to the majestic mountains towering close behind it. They were so much like the mountains in Oregon where I'd grown up and yet—

My gaze lifted to the two moons hanging in the sky. One was white and looked like "the moon," the other was a smaller pinker version. I was definitely not in Oregon anymore, or even in my own realm, and I couldn't even pretend I was.

We headed around the side of the alpha's residence which looked like an enormous Mediaeval castle complete with multiple wings and turrets and into Old Town. Unlike yesterday, Bishop took the direct path down the twisted, sloping main street and avoided the warren of narrow streets and hidden gardens. We quickly passed through the main gate in the large stone wall surrounding Stonehaven's original buildings and headed into New Town.

The hospital turned out to be a large, square building just off the main street. Its stone blocks were smaller than the blocks that made up the alpha's residence, but bigger than the buildings closer to the outskirts of town, suggesting the building wasn't hundreds of years old like Old Town, but still not new. There were also two new additions — one much newer than the other if the brick size was anything to go by — indicating that the community kept adding to its facilities as the pack's population grew.

We avoided the large courtyard with the wide doors at the front of the building that looked a lot like the entrance to the emergency area and instead entered through a modest foyer with a dozen comfortable-looking chairs and a wide reception desk.

Two young women sat behind the desk and they brightened when they saw Bishop. Then their attention slid to me. The younger of the two, a blond with short curly hair, kept her smile, while the other woman, also blond but with long hair, glowered for a split second before plastering on a smile so bright it hurt to look at her.

Yeah, Bishop had definitely left a trail of broken hearts — or hopeful hearts — behind him.

"Nova will be checking on the more serious patients," he said, nodding at the women and walking past them toward a staircase.

They both frowned as if they'd hoped he'd stop and talk— or rather flirt. I suspected if I hadn't been with him, he would have, and I had a bad feeling I was making enemies in my possibly-new pack just by being with him.

"If we can't find her at the nurses' station," he continued, "we can wait for her in the breakroom."

We went up to the second floor and down a long hall with plain white walls and a polished stone floor. It didn't have the institutional feel that hospitals in my realm had, but it was clearly designed to be practical and easily cleaned.

Wooden doors with windows lined the hall. Some stood open, some were closed, but almost all of them were for single-bed patient rooms. I didn't get a good look inside — or Bishop would have left me behind — but the equipment looked basic, suggesting this society wasn't as advanced as mine. Save for the lights, which turned on and off with a switch, nothing else indicated that they had electricity... which meant the lights were probably magical.

Men and women, mostly in loose, pale blue shirts and pants that looked a lot like scrubs, moved up and down the hall, coming and going from rooms.

We were just about to reach a T-intersection at the end of the hall when we passed a room with an enormous man in the doorway. He turned and I realized it was Finn, the pack's head of security.

His piercing blue eyes widened at seeing us then

narrowed and he stepped into the hall. "Just the man I needed to talk to," he said to Bishop.

Bishop glanced toward the T-intersection and sighed. "The nurses' station is just around the corner. I'll catch up in a minute."

"Sure." I didn't want to stand around listening to Bishop talk business with his beta, but I was still uncertain about being around strangers by myself. Hell, even being around people I knew used to be dangerous, which was why unless I'd been meeting my best friend, Mila, I'd stayed at home.

"What's she doing here?" Finn asked once I'd rounded the corner.

His voice was low and I had to strain to hear it, but the edge in his tone made me stop on the other side of the corner to listen.

I didn't know what kind of man Finn was. Sure, he might have been one of the wolves who'd saved me during the grimalkin attack, but that didn't mean he liked me, and from the sound of it, he didn't.

I also didn't know if it was worse that he'd more or less been pleasant to me during dinner the other night and hadn't shown me how he really felt or not. At least with my old pack, I knew no one liked me and they made no attempt to hide it. I couldn't risk assuming that ` because people here were polite to me, I was safe.

"I thought Nova was taking care of her at the Residence," Finn added.

"I thought I'd show her our medical facilities," Bishop

replied, his tone neutral and thankfully not announcing to the other man that we thought I might be in heat and was going to talk to Nova about birth control. Because Nova had been right. My reproductive cycle wasn't anyone's business but mine and hers and whoever I picked to get me through it.

"So now you're showing her the facilities?" Finn's tone turned exasperated. "Does Cyrus really have his sights set on her for his mate? You know the pack will never accept someone so weak."

His words stung. They shouldn't have. I hadn't been accepted before so it was foolish to think I'd be accepted now. And really! Cyrus wasn't interested in me as a mate and I wasn't interested in him... at least not for a permanent relationship.

I was smart enough to know someone like him never mated with someone like me, especially when any other woman in this pack would make a better choice.

I couldn't even fantasize about someone powerful coming along who wanted to mate with me and protect me. Not that I'd fantasized about that a lot, but Royce had made it perfectly clear when he'd faked our fated mating call and then tried to sacrifice me to a monster that no one with any kind of power would ever be interested in me.

My weakness was why Knox had rejected me right from the beginning and why he hated me so much. The weakest wolf in existence had forced a mating bond with him. I'd hate me too if I were him.

Which was logical and true and made my chest and throat tighten.

No one wanted me, and I couldn't convince myself the thought came from Knox rejecting our unwanted bond. His rejection only made the truth perfectly clear.

"Cyrus is strong enough to hold the alpha's position by himself," Bishop said, surprising me by not agreeing with Finn as well as not denying that Cyrus was interested in me becoming his mate. "He doesn't need a strong mate to help."

"But he'll lose all respect if he picks someone so weak and he'll be challenged for leadership," Finn replied, his tone shifting from anger to worry. "I'm sure once she stops looking like she's been beaten up she's cute and all, but we know nothing about her. She hasn't even shifted out her injuries, which means she's either vying for sympathy or doesn't have the strength to do a proper shift when she's hurt. Neither is good for an alpha's mate. Their pups could be powerless too and then there'd be a question of succession."

"She might be practically human," a new, masculine voice said. "But I heard she faced off with a grimalkin to protect a bunch of kids. That says something about the type of woman she is."

"Doesn't mean she'd make a good alpha's mate," Finn shot back. "Doesn't mean she'd make anyone a good mate. Would you want her to be the mother of your pups?"

"Well, I—" the new voice began.

"Of course not. No one would," Finn answered for him.

The icy hollowness inside me surged, crushing my chest. I fought to breathe as tears burned my eyes. No one wanted me. No one had ever wanted me.

The emotions are just Knox rejecting the bond. It's just Knox.

But I couldn't convince myself of that. The cold kept growing, devouring me from the inside. I was useless and weak.

Bishop and Whil had said there was a place for me here, but they were the only ones who believed that. My life in this pack wouldn't be any different than with my old pack and once my bond with Knox was broken, Cyrus and Bishop would kick me to the curb or turn me into their personal slave like Merrick had.

Except that was only if my bond with Knox could be broken and if I survived breaking it.

Maybe it would be better for everyone if I didn't survive. If I ended things now, the guys wouldn't have to risk their lives going to the death god's altar.

Maybe my father hadn't been weak when he'd taken his life. Maybe he'd just realized the truth: that everyone would be better off without him.

Except I hadn't been better off. Merrick had taken advantage of my ten-year-old naivety and used me. His son, Sterling, had used me, too. No one had been around to protect me and no one ever would.

Damn it.

Tears rolled down my cheeks and I furiously swiped them away.

I was stronger than this. I'd survived for years as the lowest of the low in my pack.

And what I felt was just the God damned bond.

I shoved away from the wall and Finn's hurtful words, not bothering to listen to the rest of the conversation. Being weak didn't mean I was helpless. I'd proven that facing off against that grimalkin — even if that grimalkin would have killed me if Knox hadn't saved me. Knox and I would break our bond, and if this pack couldn't accept me as a person then I'd find some place that would.

I'd survived almost being sacrificed to a monster. I could sure as hell survive this.

AUDREY

With my shoulders squared and my determination pushing down the grief caused by Knox rejecting the bond, I marched to the nurses' station.

An exhausted-looking nurse stood at the chest-high desk with an open folder and a pen in her hand, the pen hovering above the page as if she couldn't figure out what to write or as if she'd zoned out and forgotten what she was doing.

"I'm looking for Nova," I said. I wanted to get this conversation over with and get away from any more gossip about me before my fragile hold on my determination shattered... or before my desire returned and everyone in the building knew I needed to have sex.

The woman glanced up and opened her mouth to say something, but her expression flashed from exhausted to concerned and I gritted my teeth.

"Nova," I pressed. I hadn't looked in a mirror, but

from her reaction, it had to be obvious that I'd been crying. Past experience told me my eyes were red and my face splotchy, and I could only hope because I hadn't been crying for long, I'd look closer to normal by the time Bishop was finished talking with Finn.

That asshole who I should have told off instead of running away... and maybe if I see him again I will.

The thought shocked me and yet didn't shock me. Talking back had always ended in punishment, but so had everything else, and I guess I'd finally reached the end of my rope. I was sure I was going to cry and be a horny basket case again — and again and again — before all of this was said and done, but I also had a strange new wildness inside me. It was as if the sensation from my dreams with Knox, that I actually had a wolf buried deep in my soul, was affecting me while I was awake.

And if it got me out of this building without looking like a complete and utter mess, I didn't care if that was just my imagination or not.

"Audrey," Nova said from down the hall as she stepped out of a patient room. She wore the blue *scrubs* that everyone else was wearing even though she was the town's head physician and one of Cyrus's betas. Her light brown hair was pulled back in a ponytail and while she didn't look as exhausted as the nurse, she did look as if she'd been working with little rest since the grimalkin attack yesterday.

"Why are you out of bed?" she asked, striding to the nurses' station and setting a pile of folders on the desk.

The exhausted nurse gave her a quick nod then headed down the hall and stepped into one of the rooms.

I was supposed to stay in bed? No one had mentioned that or even tried to mention it. But of course, they were distracted with breaking my bond with Knox because Knox was their priority, not me.

"No one mentioned it," I replied. And really, I felt fine, or as fine as I could get given the circumstances.

She threw her hands up and huffed in frustration. "Why do I even bother giving them instructions? The grimalkins are a distraction, but Cyrus was clear about your... condition. He should have at least told Bishop to not let you walk all over town as if you're perfectly fine."

"My condition—?" Oh. Right. The *condition* that meant I couldn't shift and I healed more like a human than a shifter. And as much as I hadn't wanted that particular detail getting out, Nova had needed to know how to properly take care of me.

"Like I said the other night," she added. "You might look and feel fine right now, but you'll still get tired faster because your body is still processing the trauma. It's best you rest." Her attention flickered over my face but she didn't react to my red eyes or splotchy skin.

"I'll make sure she stays in bed after this," Bishop said behind me, his words instantly making me think of him naked and in bed with me.

Hot need shot straight to my core and flaming embarrassment heated my cheeks, overwhelming the last of the Finn-induced-Knox-rejecting-our-bond grief which wasn't the solution I wanted for either my emotional problems or my splotchy skin problem. Just great.

"Will that be before or after you make her march back up to the Residence?" she asked, her voice dripping with sarcasm.

"If she gets tired, I'll carry her," he replied.

My thoughts lurched to being in Bishop's arms and more heat flooded me. Both Bishop and Nova sniffed, unable to keep pretending that I wasn't flooding the hall with the scent of my arousal.

Unbelievable. Now I couldn't even get through a conversation without embarrassing myself.

"But this is important. Audrey needs to discuss her... *options*," Bishop said, his tone making options sound like a dirty word. "The sooner the better."

And now I was thinking about last night's dream and my core was trembling in anticipation. Humiliation burned my whole face, seeping into my hairline and down my neck.

"Can you please stop talking about it?" I croaked. "I'm sure Nova's already figured it out."

"Come on," Nova said, her tone softening. "We can talk in here."

She led me to the end of the hall to an empty patient room, ushered me in, and gave Bishop a "no way in hell" look when he tried to come in as well.

"Wait by the nurses' station. If Audrey wants to talk to you about it, she will." She pointed back down the hall, then shut the door in his face. "Is this your first heat? Has anyone in your family talked to you about it?"

She motioned for me to sit on the bed as she sagged onto the chair beside it.

"It's ah... It's complicated," I said.

I had no idea if I should tell her the truth, or if she'd even believe that I'd come from a different realm and heats were different there. Cyrus and Bishop hadn't believed me until Whil had confirmed it and neither of the guys had mentioned it to their betas at dinner the other night. That, and bringing it up might distract Nova from the real problem — me about to jump on any passably good-looking guy I came across — and the sooner I figured out what my options were the better. And I hoped to God they had some form of birth control here.

"Where I'm from women don't experience heats this powerful, so I'm not sure how different this will be." Not that anyone in my pack had talked about heats or that heats were an issue for any shifters in my realm. "I'm guessing it's like what I know, that I'll have a heightened sex drive for about a week, except it'll be ten times stronger." Of course, that was if what I felt was an indication of what to expect, and also assuming I actually was in heat and not just being compelled by the mating bond.

"Heats can be powerful, and from your reaction, it looks like yours is going to be pretty strong," she said. "Knowing you can't shift makes this quite unusual. The weaker shifters tend to have weaker heats so I would have though: you'd have little to no reaction. I'd like to draw some blood and run some tests."

"Will that help you figure out how I can deal with this?"

Her expression softened even more and I wondered if she thought I was younger than I really was. How old were women in this realm when they got their first heat? In my realm, it was late teens or early twenties for shifters who hadn't had their ability to shift suppressed until they were eighteen, and with my pack it was shortly after their first shift. But no matter how similar this realm was to mine, I couldn't assume anything.

"With Whil's help we've discovered lots of amazing medications, but nothing to ease the symptoms of going into heat. Because you're unmated and with the amount of pheromones you're releasing, I suggest you avoid public places until you've gotten through it, get physical contact, and—"

Need shivered down my spine and, from Nova's subtle sniff, I released another nose-full of desire.

"The contact doesn't have to be sex," she said with a soft chuckle. "Although given the strength of your symptoms already, it would probably be best. But even just increasing the amount of touching and cuddling with someone close to you will help if sex isn't the direction you want to go."

Except the only people I knew in this realm were Bishop and Cyrus and it would be a challenge to stop at just cuddling since every time Nova said the word sex I thought of them. Of course, that was if either of them were even willing to cuddle with me.

Logically, because I was a shifter, I knew my soul needed physical contact even though my wolf hadn't woken. I'd been reeling since I'd come to this realm and my body had been seriously injured twice now. Bishop placing his hand on my arm or thigh wasn't nearly enough to keep me steady. I needed more. A lot more.

Nova frowned. Guess she'd just listened to what she'd said and realized I was alone and didn't have someone to cuddle with. "When was the last time someone held you?"

Too long.

I swallowed a bitter huff. Mila had joined her mate's pack just over a year ago and before that maybe once every couple of months because Mila, once she'd become an adult, had gotten more responsibilities with her family and the pack. We hadn't really cuddled since high school which had been about five years ago.

But I'd gotten by with minimal cuddling all this time and I'd get by without significant contact now as well. I just had to wait until my soul naturally steadied... and pray nothing else happened before then to shake it.

Nova's frown deepened and a hint of her power that she'd kept tightly controlled until now rolled over me. But I didn't get the impression she was trying to make me submit. No, it felt more like she was upset and her control had slipped.

"Sorry." She pulled her power back. "From the look

on your face, I'd say it's been a while and not by your choosing."

"I didn't have much value in my previous pack and I have no family," I said, trying to keep my tone even. "So there weren't many options for cuddling."

It was just the way things were for someone so weak and there was no point in keeping it a secret. Even if I hadn't already told Cyrus and Bishop, everyone would figure it out. Hell, despite what Bishop and Whil had said, some of them, like Finn, had already decided I belonged at the bottom of the pack.

Nova's expression darkened and her power slipped her control again, sending a wave of pressure sweeping over me before she yanked it back. "Okay, since you're touch starved, I'd recommend you spend your heat at the heat clinic. Wilder and his men will be able to help you through it."

"And by helping me through it you mean...?" Was she suggesting that they have sex with me?

"I mean with you being touch starved, the best way you can get through a heat this strong is with sex. Physical contact will still help you better manage your symptoms, but in your situation, I'd say sex is the ideal."

Holy shit, she was!

She was prescribing I go have sex with a bunch of strangers.

Except if heats were a lot stronger in this realm than in mine and always had been, it made sense that their culture would develop differently and have ways of helping single women deal with it.

"The men regularly take the inhibitor extract, but just to be safe we'll get you a dose. It'll be good for four months." She stood and headed to the door. "If you don't mind Bishop coming along, we can go to the dispensary right now. If not, I can send it to your room in the Residence."

"He already knows what's happening." I huffed and hopped off the bed. "I'm sure everyone within a twenty-foot radius knows what's going on with me."

"Oh, thirty feet at least," Nova said with a chuckle and a mischievous smile, the same smile she'd had when she'd been teasing Cyrus at dinner. "It's a miracle you didn't have a trail of men following you down the street by the time you reached the hospital."

"They know they couldn't handle me," I quipped back. "I'm crazy enough to face down a grimalkin by myself."

And they didn't want to accidentally knock me up and get stuck with a pup who was just as powerless as I was.

But that was a sour, aching thought that I wasn't going to acknowledge. I'd managed to ignore the grief of Knox rejecting my bond during my conversation with Nova and if I went down the "no one wanted me" rabbit hole, I'd start crying again.

"Well, worry not. Wilder will definitely know how to handle you," she said, sending a wave of need shooting hot and heavy to my core. "I want to wait until you've had another day of healing, but I can get you set up in the clinic tomorrow and after your first session you'll be in much better control of your needs."

Except I was leaving tomorrow morning to head north to break my bond with Knox. Wilder definitely wouldn't be *handling* me.

She opened the door, wafting my scent into the hall. Bishop, who was leaning against the wall across from the door, straightened and cleared his throat. His warm brown gaze locked with mine and my pulse stuttered, my whole body aching for him.

As much as I wanted to believe I could hold myself together, my hope was quickly slipping away. Knox and I were going to have to have a conversation, and I could only hope that we could break the bond and he wouldn't try to kill one of his brothers for sleeping with me.

KNOX

Audrey stood in the center of the sacred grove, her white dress luminous in the moonlight, and I knew I was dreaming. Again.

It was the same dream I'd had every night since she'd bonded her soul with mine. She always looked stunned to be there, always so fragile even though I knew she had the willpower of any alpha if not the power, and my wolf always took over and made me rush to her side.

We crashed together like we had all the other nights, and I tangled my hand in her hair and possessed her mouth with a hunger I couldn't deny, her sweet, fresh scent mixing with her rich arousal and driving me crazy.

It was hard enough holding my wolf back and not giving in to the bond when I was awake, especially when it was obvious she was in a near-perpetual state of arousal, and it was impossible in my dreams.

"You're not going north," my wolf snarled at her as he

tore open the front of her white dress with his claws and roughly palmed her breast. "I won't let you."

"You have to," she gasped against my lips— *his* lips.

He captured her face between our hands and pulled back, glaring at her. Her brown, golden-flecked eyes locked with mine and it was as if I could see into her soul.

She ached with longing and fear just like I did and that made my wolf furious. She didn't believe him when he'd told her she belonged to us. She believed the ice I'd wrapped around our bond to keep her out was proof I didn't want her.

And I didn't. Just thinking about the bond made my pulse pick up with fear and anger. She'd trapped us. She'd fucking trapped us and going north was the only way to escape, no matter how dangerous it was for her.

"No," my wolf growled. "You're mine. He *will* submit."

The hell I will, I thought at my wolf as I tried to wrench myself away from her.

But my wolf crashed my mouth back onto Audrey's and that power hidden in the depths of her soul — that my wolf wanted to be there because this was just a dream — rolled from her body. It washed over me and my power rose to meet it.

Sparks burst around us and the need to take her, claim her, possess every part of her, surged inside me.

She tangled her fingers into my hair, her blunt human nails digging into my scalp, her body arching toward me. Her arousal clouded the air around us, heady and sweet, and my wolf plunged his fingers into her wet pussy, drawing a moan of pleasure. He didn't want fore-play, he wanted to fuck. He wanted to fuck her until she screamed his name and submitted to our bond like she'd done for the last two nights.

It was like this every dream. She had a power that surged up within her and heaved against ours, fighting me, taunting me, seducing me in a wild, primal dance of dominance. She didn't even know she was doing it even as her body submitted to us, her need driven by our unwanted mating bond—

Not the bond. She'd want us without it, my wolf said, trying to shove me further inside myself, determined to make me shut the fuck up while he fucked her. *She's ours. Always has been—*

Always will be. Yeah yeah yeah, I snarled back. *In your dreams. Which this fucking is.*

My wolf roared, inside me and out loud, and Audrey froze, her power vanishing between one rapid beat of my heart and the next, her body trembling like prey. A horrible feeling that could have only come from her through our bond swamped me, souring my desire.

She'd been in this position before. She'd been in the arms of a man, kissing him. She'd thought he loved her and he'd betrayed her. That was how she'd gotten the four ugly red scars slicing across her chest that showed up even in my dreams. That was why we'd found her in the river barely alive.

And now both my wolf and I were pissed off.

"You're mine," my wolf said, slowly inching his fingers

out of her pussy, trying to reignite her primal desire. He needed to bury our cock inside her and sink our teeth into her flesh, claiming her again and again and again. He needed to show her with our body that he would never forsake or betray her. "My mate. Mine. I won't let you sever our bond."

"You're only saying that—" Her breath hitched as my wolf brushed the pad of our thumb over her clit. "You're saying that because that's what I want you to say." A shiver rippled down her body and her long dark lashes fluttered shut. "He doesn't want me." *No one wants me.* "I'm only powerful here in this fantasy. I didn't give him a choice and I won't burden him with a mate he didn't pick himself who can't even shift."

"I chose," my wolf replied, pushing our fingers back inside her and rubbing down on her clit, our body vibrating with a need that had to be released. "I accepted the bond. I knew the truth the moment I caught your scent."

Her eyes rolled back and she arched into me, her body begging for me even if her power had yet to reignite.

"You. Are. Mine." He tightened our grip in her hair and tugged her head back.

Another shiver of anticipation swept through her and her power flickered back to life. Her eyes darkened, her pupils dilating with desire along with a hint of the wolf we could sense buried inside her, and her lips parted in invitation. But my wolf glared down at her, holding her still with our grip in her long blond hair and our fingers in her pussy, waiting.

"Knox," she breathed.

"Who do you belong to?" he demanded, our lips a breath away from hers but not touching and our fingers buried inside her, not moving, making it clear he wouldn't satisfy her until she submitted to his truth: that she was our mate.

"Please, Knox—"

"Who?" he growled, wrenching her head back farther, exposing her neck.

Her breath came in short sharp gasps, heaving her small breasts toward us, taunting us to lick and suck her, to build her up. Her hips tried to move and the scent of her arousal thickened, her need desperate. But he kept our fingers locked within her and our thumb frozen on her clit, not giving her any relief.

For fuck's sake. Give her what she needs, I snapped at him, trying to take over. She didn't deserve to be tortured like this even in my dreams. She wanted to be fucked, needed it. She needed it in real life, too, but if I wanted to break our bond, I couldn't give in to that... no matter how hard I was or how much my balls ached.

"You." Her power rolled up from the depths of her being, fighting her submission to us, and slammed into me more powerful than the previous dreams.

A deep gong sounded, reverberating through me, making the ice I'd woven around my heart and the magical chain binding our souls together tremble.

My pants vanished — because this was a dream — and my cock sprung free.

"You, Knox. I belong to you."

I needed to be buried inside her. I needed to hear her scream my name.

Fuck my wolf and fuck this dream.

"Always," my wolf replied as *I* — not my wolf — captured her lips in a wild, possessive kiss.

I claimed her mouth, desperate and hungry for something I'd never had before and never wanted until now: acceptance.

I didn't know if the real Audrey would ever be able to accept someone like me, someone who would rather be a wolf, who didn't like crowds or, hell, even people, and someone who couldn't stand to be in my own bedroom in the Residence because the room was too small. But it didn't matter. This was a dream. She'd submitted to my claim which meant for this brief moment she accepted me. And from the way she kissed me back and held on to my head, keeping me close, she craved me as well.

I pushed my fingers in and out of her, building her up. Her channel was slick and hot, and her hips rocked into my hands, her body perfectly matching this wild primal dance between us. It was driving me crazy imagining what it was going to feel like to push into her, but even in my dreams she was tight, and I didn't want to hurt her. I wanted her boneless and soaking wet when I took her. I wanted every nerve ignited so she felt every inch of me.

"Knox," she moaned, a shiver rolling from her head to

her pussy, her inner muscles fluttering around my fingers. "Mate."

The word shot like lightning straight to my cock. I ground my thumb down on her clit and pushed her over the edge. Her muscles clamped around my fingers, but I kept sliding them in and out of her, drawing out the tremors.

"Oh, fuck," she gasped, her body twitching, her hips riding my hand, greedy for every last drop of pleasure, and this time, unlike last night — because I was in charge and not my wolf— I waited until she was done before impaling her on my cock.

"Oh, fuck," she groaned again, as I pressed her back against the soft, mossy ground, and pushed inside her.

Her muscles still fluttered around me, her hot slickness easing just enough of the pressure and friction so I could smoothly bury myself to the hilt in one powerful stroke. Fuck, she felt so good, so perfect. So mine.

I sucked in breaths heavy with her arousal and her sweet scent, my balls aching, pausing to savor the feel of her. Her power crackled against mine, bright golden sparks flickering at the edge of my vision and teasing along my spine. Her brown eyes were slightly glazed with pleasure, her expression was pure bliss. A soft golden glow radiated from her skin and once again she looked like the goddess I'd glimpsed when she been fighting that grimalkin. Except now, instead of a warrior goddess, she was a goddess of desire.

"Mine," my wolf said and her face lit up with a brilliant smile.

Until we set her free, I whispered to myself then I gave myself over to my wolf and my primal need.

We pumped in and out of her, picking up speed, stealing her gasps and mewls with our kisses, and turning them into moans of pleasure. Her body and power crashed against ours, driving us wild, but somehow we managed to hold ourselves together until her whole body tensed with another orgasm and she screamed my name. Then we lost it, hammering into her, chasing our own release, until we exploded inside her.

Her pussy milked us, greedily contracting around our cock, drawing out both of our orgasms, and my wolf preened with satisfaction.

Our mate was happy and satisfied and our mating bond was even stronger.

My pulse stuttered.

Oh, fuck. The ice around the chain binding us together had cracks in it and the chain itself was bigger and thicker.

I told her you'd accept her, my wolf said, his smug satisfaction souring the afterglow of coming.

I haven't accepted her, I snarled back. This was just a dream, a fantasy, a way to relieve the pressure of the mating bond. I didn't want a mate. I couldn't be trapped like that.

You did accept her. You fucked her this time, not me.

I stared down where my cock was buried inside her.

Fuck me. My damned wolf was right. I hadn't just been a passenger like I'd been the previous two nights. Tonight I'd taken control and claimed her... and I had a horrible feeling that even though this was a dream, I'd just made our real bond that much harder to break and that much harder to resist.

CYRUS

I stood in the courtyard outside the Residence with Deacon and his all-female hunt team, glaring at the brightening eastern horizon and trying to keep my power under control.

Yesterday, Bishop had told me he'd overheard Nova tell Audrey to spend her heat with Wilder, and my wolf had lost his shit. It had been a struggle to get through the rest of the day without flattening everyone around me with my power and even more of a struggle last night to keep my wolf under control and not march us to Audrey's bedroom and give her what she needed.

My wolf snarled at me, still pissed that I hadn't given in to *that* desire.

Nova had told Audrey to go to Wilder. Wilder of all people!

It didn't matter that he was experienced and sensitive and the best man for the job. My wolf refused to accept that Audrey had to go to some other man to satisfy her blatantly obvious needs and was furious that I wouldn't give him a chance to take care of her.

Fuck! It was ridiculous.

My wolf had never cared what the women in our lives did, even the handful of women we'd had somewhat serious relationships with. We weren't jealous. So long as everyone talked about it and agreed, multiple partners weren't a problem. My brothers and I had grown up with two dads and there were a number of multi-partner matings in town so it wasn't unheard of.

It also wasn't like Wilder was going to mate with her. He or one of his guys — or all of them if she so desired — we're going to help her get through the overwhelming need of her heat. He'd treated tons of women before and he'd continue to treat them until he decided to retire. Audrey would just be another patient.

But I couldn't convince my wolf of that, and I couldn't even convince myself that my reaction was because it was obvious Bishop was falling for her or that she might have to become Knox's mate if we couldn't break the mating bond.

She was suffering and *I* needed to take care of her.

I gritted my teeth and mentally clenched harder at my power. I had to stay in control and not let myself be distracted by a woman I couldn't have, even if I actually wanted her... which I didn't, damn it.

As much as I didn't want Nova to be right about who I could take as a mate, she was. I'd already heard whispers about how weak Audrey was while making my rounds and informing our betas that the three of us were leaving to take Audrey north. I'd also gotten a number of concerned looks and outright objections, particularly from Velora and Finn.

It seemed the rumor mill was determined to believe I wanted Audrey even though I *knew* mating with her would cause problems.

Which was ridiculous. Hadn't they seen how Bishop couldn't stop staring at her at dinner or that she'd been shopping with Bishop the other day, not me? How had they jumped to the conclusion I wanted her as my mate and not Bishop?

But the bigger problem was that my wolf didn't give a fuck that they thought she wouldn't make a good mate. She'd been willing to risk everything to save pups. It didn't matter if she had power or not, that made her perfect.

Except that didn't necessarily make an ideal alpha, and if I took Audrey as my mate, she'd become the pack alpha with me, and without power, it would be a constant battle to have people respect her and not challenge us for leadership.

Whil hurried around the side of the Residence, her small travel pack hanging at her hip, the strap slung across her chest. "I'm sorry. I couldn't decide which book I might need more."

"We're still waiting on Bishop and Audrey," I replied.

Whil's gaze swept over the group. "Knox?"

"He's waiting just outside the Residence's walls." Before Audrey, he would have been in the courtyard, close to the hunt team, although still not a part of the group. But now, he couldn't even be near that many people, even if half of the people were wolves.

Bishop had mentioned yesterday that Knox was becoming more withdrawn and he was worried. His twin had a stranglehold on their twin bond and the most Bishop was getting from Knox was his desire for Audrey. He wasn't even getting anger or fear anymore and those were usually the emotions Knox couldn't hide from Bishop.

Do you want me to send Lyra to get them, Deacon asked in my head.

But the front door opened before I could respond, and Bishop and Audrey hurried out dressed to travel and carrying their packs.

"My fault," Audrey murmured, her cheeks flushing and her gaze dropping to her feet making it obvious her heat had been what had delayed her. "I'm trying to get it under control."

I glanced at Bishop. His expression was pinched and he gave a slight shake of his head in response to my silent question. She hadn't turned to him for help. She was still trying to deal with it alone.

My wolf heaved under my skin at that thought and a whisper of my power slip my mental grasp.

"I'll control it," she insisted, mistaking my released

power as anger at her inability to control a bodily function that could be hard to control at the best of times.

And is impossible right now because she's touch starved, my wolf snarled at me.

Which was information Nova had snapped at me when I'd gone to her for extra elixirs and medical supplies and told her we were taking Audrey north.

But it wasn't something I could wait out or do anything about. We had to get to the death god's altar before Knox and Audrey lost their minds or had sex and sealed a bond neither of them wanted. The best we could do would be to try to find time to hold her without succumbing to her scent... because I had a horrible feeling once my wolf got a taste of her, he was never letting her go.

The image of my face buried between her thighs jumped into my mind.

Fuck me.

"Stay downwind," I said, clamping down on those thoughts.

With a snarl, I swung my travel pack onto my shoulder. It was stuffed with my supplies and Knox's — since he'd probably spend most of this trip in his wolf form — and wasn't heavy enough to weigh me down, but that meant it wasn't a distraction from my wolf's thoughts about what it wanted me to do with Audrey.

"Eyes open for grimalkins," I barked, striding toward the front gate. "Deacon, you and your team lead the way."

Deacon, a large gray wolf, bounded in front of me,

and the rest of his team, four sleek brown wolves, followed. Ahead of them, a large black shadow slipped down the road, keeping to the shadows and as far away from Audrey as his unwanted bond would let him.

Thankfully we were up early enough that there weren't a lot of people around to see our group marching down the sloping twisted streets and heading out on the main road toward the last patrol shed. Unfortunately, I knew we hadn't left unnoticed and the rumors that Bishop and I had left with Whil, a hunt team, and Audrey, would spread through town before sunset.

I hadn't thought taking care of Audrey in our residence and introducing her to our betas would be enough to start rumors, but it had been, and I could only imagine what the rumors were going to be by the time we got back.

Which really, was so low on my list of things to worry about it was ridiculous that I was even thinking about them now.

But there were only two things I could do on the long walk to patrol shed twelve: keep my eyes open from trouble, something Deacon's team was already doing, and think. And because the walk was slower than I wanted — because Whil and Audrey didn't have the stamina of a wolf — we needed to watch our pace. And that gave me far too much time to think.

Really, I should be thinking about the grimalkins and how they'd slipped past our hunt teams and territory patrol teams as well as the town's watch or why Jundar had called an emergency meeting of the Mountain and Sea Alliance because of increased beast activity in neighboring areas. Except my thoughts kept jumping back to Audrey.

Audrey who needed someone to protect her and nurture her confidence. She'd faced off against a grimalkin, she'd survived the horrible ordeal that had brought her to our realm, she had the soul of a fighter, but it was buried deep within her, just like her wolf... just like my wolf wanted to be.

And now I was thinking about sex again. Wonderful.

AUDREY

WE WALKED ALL MORNING, TOOK A QUICK BREAK AT LUNCH for water and a handful of rations — since wolf shifters with an awakened wolf could live on one meal a day if they needed to — and walked for the rest of the afternoon.

After we'd left town, Deacon and his hunt team had spread out into the tall grass, searching the area for trouble and letting Cyrus and Whil take the lead, while Knox remained out of sight.

I'd hung back — and downwind from Cyrus — with Bishop. By his sniff and the darkening of his eyes the moment I'd opened my door this morning, he'd known I'd done some serious masturbating in an attempt to ease the aching desire of my heat, or my mating bond, or whatever the hell it was that was driving me crazy.

Thankfully, he hadn't commented on it then and didn't bring it up during our walk. Instead, he talked about safe stuff like the pack's territory and trade with a seaport on the other side of the mountain.

My feet had been sore when we'd stopped for lunch and they, along with my legs, were killing me by the time we stopped at a wooden shed forty feet off the road. Hell, all of me was sore. My pack that hadn't been heavy at the beginning of the day now weighed a ton and I was hungry and exhausted, and we'd only been walking for one day!

I had no idea how I was going to make it the nine days it was going to take to get to the death god's altar.

Except I was just going to have to. Cyrus was already pissed at me. It would be better to prove I wasn't completely pathetic and figure out how to pull my own weight on this journey. I wouldn't be able to help in a fight, but I could still—

God, I had no idea what I could offer. I'd never camped before, had no idea how to start a fire without a lighter or a match, and didn't know the flora well enough to scavenge for food to help make our rations last.

It looked like the only thing I could do right now was keep up, follow any orders Cyrus gave me, and not complain.

"Drop your pack in the shed, grab the bucket just inside the door, and draw water from the well for the hunt team," Cyrus said to me.

"Right." I trudged to the wooden structure and opened the door.

The shed was... a shed. One door and no windows. It

was a fifteen-by-fifteen wooden structure that was smaller on the inside because of trunks and shelves and a tall rack filled with firewood along the back wall and left-hand corner. The ground was hardpacked dirt, which wasn't comfortable but safer than a wooden floor, and there was a small hearth and fieldstone chimney against the righthand wall.

I found the bucket, grabbed it, and set my pack where it had been, then headed to the well a few feet away.

Cyrus still stood on the road with Whil beside him, scanning the sea of grass and wildflowers all around us. He said something to her, too quiet for me to hear, and she nodded, her attention locked on something far off in the distance.

Their expressions were grim, but I didn't know if it was because of what we were planning on doing, the grimalkins that had attacked the town the other day, or the strange magic the hunt team had found.

And really, it didn't matter. I doubted they'd tell me, and even if they did, I wouldn't be able to help. The most I could do was follow Cyrus's instructions and draw water for the hunt team... whatever that meant.

I went to the old-fashioned well, complete with a rope-bucket pully system, and drew up a bucketful of water then dumped it into the bucket I'd taken from the shed. I wasn't sure what else I was supposed to do with the water and was on the verge of asking Bishop — who was building a fire in a firepit halfway between the shed and the road — when one of the sleek brown hunt team members came out of the grass, dropped a dead rabbit at Cyrus's feet, and went straight to my bucket. She murmured a *thanks* in my head and drank deeply then headed back into the grass.

Bishop got the fire going, Cyrus took the rabbit and thankfully headed away from the shed into the waist-high grass to skin and gut it where I couldn't see, while the other hunt members visited my bucket and drank.

I wasn't sure what else to do so I made sure the "drinking" bucket was always full. But it was a hurry up and wait kind of job and the exhaustion from walking all day sank into my body and mind, dragging me into a heavy numbness.

Around me, the breeze, starting to cool as the sun set, ruffled my hair and made the tall grasses *shush*.

Stillness.

Shush.

Stillness.

Shush.

The icy hollowness dimmed and so, too, did my achy need as if I was softly separating from my body.

A flurry of birds that looked a little like sparrows but not quite took off from the grass stalks, tugging me back to myself, strengthening all my unwanted emotions. They chattered with each other and scolded whatever had disturbed them then flew away, leaving a heavy, peaceful near silence in their wake.

I'd only experienced the near-silence a few times before since the only place I'd been able to find it had been in the heart of my old pack's forest and it usually hadn't been safe to be there.

There was an energy in the silence, a gentle vibration that filled the air and called to me.

It said I belonged, that I was home.

There was too much noise everywhere else, too much energy from others. But in the silence, I could feel my primal connection with nature and could imagine that connection came from the wolf asleep inside me.

I let my mind and body drift again and the gentle vibration changed, my senses zeroing in on a ferocious feral power. It was just a whisper, his power was fully contained, yet somehow I could still sense it.

Of course, my soul would always sense it, would always be drawn to it, and would always recognize it.

Because he was my mate and every fiber of my being believed he always would be.

Knox.

I hadn't even caught a glimpse of him all day and I knew if I turned around to look, he'd stay hidden in the grass.

The icy hollowness and the grief of rejection fluttered in my chest along with my achy need to seal our bond, but the sensations didn't overwhelm me, and I'd never been so happy in my life to be too exhausted to feel anything.

"Audrey," Cyrus barked.

I jerked, my eyes flying open. I hadn't even realized I'd closed them.

"Fill up the bucket and bring it." He strode past me and headed into the grass away from our makeshift campground.

The bucket was already full, so I picked it up and followed him.

He turned so the breeze was at his back — reminding me that he didn't want to catch the scent of my uncontrolled desire — squatted and held out his bloody hands.

"I didn't get a chance to talk to you before we left," he said his voice gruff as I hefted the bucket and poured a stuttering stream of water onto his hands so he could wash them.

My heart did a strange flipflop that I attributed to my perpetual state of semi-arousal. Maybe he wasn't as angry at me as I thought. Gruff did seem to be his natural state. Even during the dinner with his betas where he'd lightened up a bit — mostly because Nova kept teasing him — he was still kind of surly. Maybe I could actually trust him not to turn on me the second my bond with Knox was broken and that there was a place for me among his pack that didn't involve me being a slave.

"You can't fight and you can't shift, so I doubt you can hunt," he said, crushing the flicker of hope I'd had that he thought I was actually worth something. "How different is our realm from yours? Would you be able to tell what plant is and isn't poisonous?"

I wouldn't have been able to tell what plant was poisonous back home. "Probably not, but I—"

"I'm guessing the stars are different, too," he said,

cutting me off before I could say I could learn. "If they were the same, would you know how to find your way back to town?"

"No."

His eyes narrowed and a hint of his power rolled over me. "How basic do I need to go? If you don't have a starter, can you start a fire?"

That was basic? I was pretty sure most people didn't know how to start a fire without a lighter or match. Sure, they'd probably seen the stick thing on TV before, but I doubt they'd tried it and I had a feeling it was a lot harder than the movies made it out to be. But that was my realm. Maybe every child here learned how to start a fire without a starter in preschool.

His gaze bore into me, his wolf rising to the surface and darkening his eyes, reminding me that in this situation, I was prey and he was the predator. Hell, in every situation I was prey.

"What *can* you do?" he growled, the pressure from his power growing, demanding I answer him.

But as he so aptly pointed out, I couldn't fight and I couldn't hunt. In this situation, there wasn't anything I could do. I didn't know anything about surviving in the wild. I hadn't even watched any of those survival TV shows. If we were back in the town though—

I thought about what I could and couldn't do that didn't involve creating a spreadsheet for a computer they didn't have or writing an essay on a history that didn't exist in this realm. My possible list of skills was far too short. All I could really do was clean and cook, and I wasn't sure my cooking skill would be helpful in this situation since I'd never cooked over a campfire before. Hell, I couldn't even read and write anymore since I didn't know this world's language and the magic that let me understand them and be understood only worked with verbal communication.

The thought made me sad and frustrated. What had I been doing with my life? Nothing. Not a damn thing.

No.

I shoved those feelings as deep down as I could before they fully woke the grief from Knox rejecting our bond.

I wasn't lazy or stupid. I hadn't been *allowed* to do anything.

"Anything?" he pressed, his power compelling me to answer.

"No." My throat tightened and my grief gained strength despite my determination to ignore it.

Damn it. There had to be something I could do. I couldn't be completely useless.

Except, right here and now, I was.

"There's nothing," I forced out.

Cyrus grunted and straightened, glowering down at me as if he'd suspected what my answer would be and still didn't like it.

"The first few rabbits should be ready soon," he said and took the mostly empty bucket from me and strode back to the well. He refilled it then headed to the campfire and sat.

I stared at his broad, straight back, fighting to regain control of my emotions before following him. But I was exhausted and the best I could manage was to hold back my tears. Because damn it, I was *not* going to cry just because Cyrus, like everyone else in my life, had pointed out I was useless.

I should have been used to it by now. Sterling and his friends had reminded me almost every day that I was worthless. But no one knew me here and a part of me had hoped even though I was next to powerless and couldn't shift that the shifters here would see me in a different light.

With a sigh, I waded out of the tall grass to the hard-packed earth and stone area where Bishop, Cyrus, Whil, and two wolves — one of them Deacon — sat around the campfire. Two rabbits had been skewered on a long metal stick which was propped up by metal stands on either side, creating a rotisserie, and the smell of roasting meat wafted over me.

"Here," Whil said as I approached, and she dipped a metal cup into the water bucket and held it out to me.

"Thanks." I took the cup and scanned the area for a place to sit, preferably away — and hopefully downwind — from Cyrus.

"Come," Bishop said, patting the ground beside him. "Sit with me."

AUDREY

I TOOK THE CUP, TRUDGED THE REMAINING FEW FEET TO Bishop, and sagged to the ground, finally off my feet. But before I could settle, he grabbed me around the waist and hauled me into his lap.

"What are you doing?" I asked, my voice suddenly breathy as soft, sensual need swept through me.

"Before we left, Nova reminded me that I'm an idiot," he replied, his breath feathering across my skin.

A shiver of desire swept through me, but thankfully I was too exhausted, and it wasn't strong enough to compel me to beg him to have sex with me. Except that didn't stop my mind from jumping to the dreams I'd been having where Knox — looking like a moodier version of Bishop — made me come with screaming satisfaction, or remembering the look in Bishop's eyes the other day when I'd stepped out of my bedroom. He'd looked almost as hungry as dream-Knox with his wolf-darkened eyes.

My attention flickered across the fire to Cyrus, my fantasy sliding to him. I'd actually seen him naked and knew just how perfect and powerful his body was. His gaze caught mine, but his expression didn't change, as if he didn't have any feelings about his brother holding me... or was hiding them. There wasn't even a hint of power and I didn't know if that meant he approved or if he didn't want to start a fight.

"You've suffered two traumatic events in the last few days and you don't have anyone here to help steady your soul." He pressed on my shoulders, urging me to lie back against his chest even though I was sure he could smell my increased arousal.

His length hardened against my butt.

Oh yeah, he could smell it.

"You'll be better able to manage your heat if your soul is steady."

I moved to look him in the eyes, shifting my rear against him and making his breath hitch. "I'm not sure this is a good idea."

Need made his eyes even darker, but his expression was tight as if he was determined to control himself. "I'm not going to take advantage of you," he murmured. "I'll keep you safe. I promise."

His words swirled more heated desire into my chest, but on top of that— No it was *stronger than* that, there was something else, something softer but just as enveloping. It was like the energy I'd felt earlier by the well while embracing the near silence whispering in my heart: connected, safe, home.

I'd never experienced anything like it before. The sensation wasn't strong, but it was there, a ghost in my cells, a vibration that called to the wolf nature I feared I didn't really have, a foundation that would support me.

"What is this?" I breathed, pressing my hand over my heart.

"Our shifter connection," Bishop replied.

But that was impossible. Cuddling with Mila had never felt like this, and while those closer to each other, like mates and siblings, had stronger connections, close friends could have just as strong a connection.

Except perhaps a stronger shifter connection was just another magical thing that was different in this realm.

"Come," he murmured, urging me to relax and fully accept his embrace. "It'll help. I promise."

With a sigh, I gave in and leaned back. Distracting, achy need aside, it felt good to have his arms around me, and I was just too tired to fight him or do much of anything about our mutual attraction.

I turned my attention to the fire, watching it flicker and sway in the soft breeze, and let myself drift on the warmth of my shifter connection with Bishop. My eyelids fluttered closed and the exhaustion of the day sank deeper into my bones.

"Hey," Bishop said, taking my water cup — that I was about to dump in my lap — and setting it on the ground.

"You need to stay awake until you eat something. Talk to me, tell me something about yourself."

"You already know the gist of it." I didn't want to talk about myself. As Cyrus had proven, my life had been simple and secluded, and the only other thing of note he and Bishop didn't know was how I was the one who found my father in the bathtub after he killed himself. And I really didn't have the emotional strength to bring that up. "There isn't much else."

"I'm sure there are lots, like ... have you ever seen an angel?"

Cyrus grunted, took the rabbits off the spit, and speared two more. I wasn't sure what the grunt meant. Bishop had been curious about angels — about my whole realm actually — and Cyrus had shut his questions down because they'd had more important things to worry about at the time.

"I haven't seen one in person," I told Bishop, "but I've seen them on TV."

"TV? What's that?" Whil asked, gingerly picking apart the rabbits and distributing the pieces among four metal bowls.

"It's—" How could I explain it? I didn't think they had electricity and I had no idea what level of technology they did have, not to mention if any of my realm's technology had a magical replacement in this realm.

"Do you have photography?" I asked. Bishop frowned. Maybe the realm's magic couldn't translate the word like it hadn't with TV. "It's a way of capturing an image on a specially treated—" Hmm, I couldn't say film. If they didn't know the word photography, they probably wouldn't understand *film* in that context. "—a specially treated piece of paper?"

"No," he replied, as Whil handed us our bowls of roasted rabbit.

Okay, so... I guess it would be best to just really simplify it. I picked up a piece of meat and blew on it to cool it off while trying to figure out the best way to explain it, but it was a struggle to focus and keep my eyes open.

"Well... we have... devices that let us capture images. Still ones, like a picture, and moving ones like a play."

"How is this related to this TV?" Cyrus asked, his voice jolting me as if I'd been on the verge of falling asleep. His gaze met mine, dipped to my hands then rose again. "Eat."

Right. Food. I really *was* hungry, but eating just seemed like too much work, and Bishop's embrace was so warm and relaxing and—

"Eat," Cyrus insisted, and a soft wave of his power jolted me awake again and made me pop a piece of meat into my mouth before I fully realized what I was doing.

"You don't have to force me," I said.

"Kind of looks like I do," Cyrus replied. "I'm going to keep waking you up until you've finished what you've been given."

Another soft wave of power made me eat more of my dinner and I glowered at him.

Cyrus met my glare, his expression smug and cocky, which did nothing to diminish his attractiveness. In fact, that cocky confidence and smirk that said he knew he didn't even need to use a fraction of his power to make me submit only made him more attractive.

"Now tell Bishop about this TV before he dies from curiosity," he said.

"What, no power? Not going to force me to tell him?" I huffed and popped more meat in my mouth before he made me do it.

"Do I need to?" he growled, sending a shiver of need rushing through me.

Oh, yes—

No! No no no. My body might have thought Cyrus making me submit was exactly what I wanted, but it wasn't. What I really wanted was to feel his power like I felt Knox's power in my dreams, not controlling me, but awakening that wild and primal something within me.

He quirked an eyebrow, a whisper of his power teasing over me.

"The TV?" Bishop prompted.

I wrenched my attention away from Cyrus before my desire overwhelmed me. I liked being in Bishop's arms, liked the warmth and comfort and sense of *home,* and I didn't want to ruin it by trying to rip his clothes off and have him take me while everyone around the campfire watched.

"We watch the images we've captured on the TV." I

finished off my meat, but Bishop took my bowl and replaced it with his which was still full.

"That's not fair."

"I can eat later," he murmured. "But you're not going to last for the next two rabbits to finish cooking."

"Fine," I grumbled, shoving more meat into my mouth before Cyrus could command me. "I've seen the angels in the Joined Parliament and I've also seen footage from the war of angels fighting Michael's nephilim."

The fire snapped and I realized I was starting to drift off again.

"Do you miss it?" Bishop asked.

I finished my mouthful but the idea of moving my hand to pluck more meat out of the bowl and eat suddenly seemed exhausting.

"I really miss cars," I sighed. How was I going to handle another day of straight walking, let alone eight more days after that?

BISHOP

AUDREY'S EYES SLID SHUT AND SHE WENT LIMP IN MY ARMS, fast asleep. My bowl started to slide from her fingers, and I caught it and set it on the ground before she spilled it.

Aaaaand she's out, Deacon said in my head with a chuckle. *I'm actually surprised you didn't have to force her to stay awake to eat, too.*

Cyrus grunted at that, probably pissed that he'd been forced to make her eat in the first place. He didn't like to use his power like that, but she'd been falling asleep before the rabbits had even finished cooking and, like me, he probably doubted she'd stay awake long enough to start dinner let alone finish it.

How much did she manage to eat? he asked, his tone clear that if he didn't think she'd eaten enough, he'd wake her again.

Not enough considering we walked all day and are going

to walk most of the day tomorrow. She sighed and shifted against my rock-hard cock, snuggling closer.

I gritted my teeth and fought to keep my promise to her. Just because I said I wasn't going to do anything didn't mean I didn't want to. And with her delicious, seductive scent filling the air around me, it was getting harder by the minute — my cock as well as the effort to resist.

We can put the leftover rabbit in some oatmeal in the morning, I said, trying to keep my mental voice calm and not give away how much she was affecting me. I was sure it was obvious to everyone that I was attracted to her, but I didn't want Cyrus to worry about me being distracted. He had enough to worry about already.

Deacon, still in his wolf form because he and his hunt team would remain as wolves for the entire hunt unless necessary, stared at me.

You sure you want to take her north? From her scent, she's only days away from a full heat. His golden gaze dipped to her and I instinctively tightened my grip. My wolf and I *needed* to protect her even if Deacon wasn't a threat.

It was obvious she was struggling with the journey already even though she hadn't complained. After lunch, her pace kept getting slower and slower and her gait had become uneven. Without a doubt, if she wasn't in pain now, she would be in the morning.

With the strength of her heat already, I doubt just holding her is going to be enough to get her through, Deacon added.

It might be more effective than you think, Cyrus replied.

Deacon snorted. *That sounds like wishful thinking. You best make your situation clear to her so she doesn't get the wrong idea.*

She won't be getting the wrong idea, Cyrus growled. *I'm not sleeping with her.* He turned to me and frowned. *Did you see her reaction to your soul steadying hers? It's like she's never been held before.* A ripple of power slipped his control, revealing his frustration, and he yanked the last two rabbits from the spit. *We deal with that and she'll be fine.*

I doubt that, Deacon huffed. *If no one has held her before, she'd be insane— well, more insane than whatever that fantasy tale was that she was telling Bishop, so someone has obviously held her. Jeez, Cyrus, this isn't like you.*

Would everyone stop telling me what I think or feel, he snarled back. *I haven't suddenly forgotten my duty to the pack.*

Then why the hell do the three of you have to be the ones to personally see her home? Deacon demanded.

Cyrus growled and I clenched my jaw. Knox had been adamant about not telling anyone other than Whil what had happened, but given that we were going north into dangerous lands, Deacon wasn't going to be happy with a "just because" explanation.

He'd probably also been hounded by Nova to get the truth before we parted ways tomorrow afternoon. And while those two were the most laid-back betas on our team, they were the least likely to accept "just because."

Fuck, Knox snarled in my head. He wasn't as involved

in the day-to-day running of the pack, but he still knew our betas and knew Deacon wasn't going to give up. *We're not taking her home. Somehow she mate bonded with me without either of us saying the vows and Whil thinks there's a way in the northern death god's realm to break it without killing either of us.*

Deacon's gaze jumped to mine then across the fire to Cyrus. *You're shitting me.*

Cyrus met his stare.

The fire crackled and popped then popped again.

Holy fuck! He burst out laughing, his wolf chuffing while his mental voice roared through our heads. *That's god-level fucked up. If she was going to manipulate any of you with a love potion, she should have targeted you,* he said, looking at me. *Out of all the guys she could have picked. Fuck! She picked Knox?*

She didn't pick me, Knox snarled back. *It just happened.*

"Likely a nasty side-effect of the magic that brought her to this realm," Whil whispered, loud enough for us to hear but soft enough to not wake Audrey since she didn't have telepathy like we did.

This realm? She's from a different one? Well, that explains the weird conversation you had, he said excepting Whil's explanation without hesitation. *Oh, Great Sisters, that poor girl. Mated to Knox.* Deacon's laughter abruptly stopped. *Shit. No wonder her heat is driving her crazy. You haven't sealed the bond.*

"That's part," Whil replied. "But given that she's said heats in her realm aren't powerful, I suspect there's something about this realm affecting her. It could be the same with soul-steadying touch. Which means she might not need as much touch because of where she's from, or she'll need more because this realm is changing her and she's already at a deficit."

Sisters! She just couldn't catch a break. Abused, betrayed, thrown into an unfamiliar realm, and mate bonded with someone who didn't want her, and now that bond and this realm were changing her body in unexpected ways.

She's going to need help adapting, I said only to Cyrus and Knox. *If holding her isn't enough, I can take care of her. You don't have to worry about her getting the wrong idea. Knox—?* I shouldn't have needed to ask his permission, and he was smart enough to figure out I was going to have sex with Audrey if she needed it, but I needed to know he'd be able to control himself if or when that happened.

Do whatever the fuck you want, he snarled. *I don't care.*

A sliver of anger seeped past the block he'd put on our twin bond, but it was too slight for me to figure out if he was pissed at the idea of me having sex with her or pissed at himself.

Don't get attached, Cyrus added. *We can't forget that this might not end well. If it comes down to her or Knox, I'm picking Knox.*

You don't have to remind me. I know our priorities. Except telling him that made my wolf heave inside me.

We loved Knox. He was our other half, and even

though he was actively trying to keep me out right now, we were and always would be connected.

But even though there was a risk his wolf would take over and go feral, he was still stronger than Audrey. And keeping Audrey safe, even if it meant having to convince Knox to accept their mating bond, was the best way to keep Knox safe.

And she's going to need more than just help, Cyrus added, more of his power slipping, his worry about the situation growing. *She can't fight or hunt or start a fire.*

Audrey groaned but didn't wake, and I glared at Cyrus. *Control yourself, she needs her sleep.*

She needs a fucking miracle, Cyrus shot back. *She can't do anything.*

My wolf, already dangerously close to the surface because I was holding Audrey, wrenched free and took over.

Don't you dare say that where she can hear it, my wolf snarled at him. *Her sense of self-worth is fragile and Knox rejecting their bond isn't helping. If she's never been held and she now needs it to the same degree we do, her emotional state is even more precarious.*

I know, Cyrus growled back, his power flickering then vanishing before it could affect her again. *She's going to be exhausted, but we need to teach her everything we can. If she gets separated from us, she won't survive.*

She won't get separated, my wolf snarled back.

You can't guarantee that, Cyrus said, his wolf taking

over as well and glaring back at me. *We protect her by making her stronger.*

Agreed, I replied.

Agreed, Knox's wolf whispered through our twin bond so softly I wasn't sure Knox was aware his wolf had spoken.

AUDREY

I woke alone in the windowless shed. Someone, probably Bishop, had brought me inside and covered me with a blanket, and from the light leaking around the door, it looked like I'd slept all night and into the morning.

With a groan I sat up. My legs and feet throbbed from walking all day yesterday while the rest of me throbbed from yet another sexy dream.

Like before, Knox had pounced on me like I was his favorite meal, and I'd gone from those initial first moments of confusion to wet and ready in a heartbeat — thank you dreams!

This time, he'd lifted me up, pinned my back against a tree trunk, and brought me down onto his cock in one fast powerful stroke. As usual, all I could do was hold on for the ride and submit to the pleasure, so I'd wrapped my legs around his waist and let him pound into me until stars burst across my vision and his cum exploded into me.

The memory sent a miniature climax shuddering through me and a sensual moan escaped my lips.

I pulled the blanket over my head and groaned. I'd hoped I was too tired for another sexy dream or that somehow leaving the town would help, but nope. Exhaustion or change of location didn't matter, and, like all the times before, I woke only partially satisfied and aching to give myself a little more.

Except I should probably practice a little self-restrained. After today, I wouldn't have privacy. I'd be out in the open, camping under the stars with the guys and I couldn't just give myself an orgasm with them watching.

The thought of Bishop and Cyrus with hungry, wolf-darkened eyes and hard cocks watching Knox push into me sent another miniature climax rushing through me.

Oh, fuck.

I *liked* that idea.

What was wrong with me?

The mating bond was urging me to have sex with Knox and I was in heat. I had to be. *That* was what was wrong with me.

There was no point in hiding it or feeling ashamed. As soon as one of them opened the shed door, or as soon as I stepped out, they were going to smell that I was just as achy and desperate this morning as I was yesterday morning and the morning before that. And if I was going to get through this journey without begging Bishop or

Cyrus to sleep with me or giving in and sealing my bond with Knox, I was going to have to relieve the pressure.

I pushed my hand down the front of my pants and ran my finger through my folds. I was so wet I had to have come in my sleep, and I was still strung so tight, I came almost the second I rubbed my slickened finger over my clit.

Jeez, we couldn't get to this death god's altar soon enough.

I gave myself two orgasms, hoping it would be enough to take the edge off, then squared my shoulders, my cheeks hot with embarrassment despite my determination to not be ashamed, and stepped out of the shed.

All the men instantly turned to look at me, even Deacon, still in his wolf form, who stood forty feet away on the road. Swell.

My embarrassment burned hotter, searing over my whole face and sweeping down my neck. But I made myself march to the fire, checked the direction of the smoke, and sat downwind from Cyrus.

"It's going to take half the day to reach Anakar," Cyrus said, not addressing my obvious arousal, his attention locked on the pot hanging from the rotisserie over the fire. "We'll make sure Whil and the hunt team are set, then carry on."

I nodded as Whil scooped what looked like oatmeal out of the pot into a bowl, added a spoon, and handed it to me.

"I want to get as far away from Darkweald as possible

before we stop for the night," he continued, still not looking at me.

"I understand," I said even though I wasn't a hundred percent sure he was talking to me.

"Good." He stood and dumped the bucket of water on the fire. "You've got ten minutes."

"Good morning to you, too," I mumbled to his back as he strode away. His shoulders stiffened, obviously hearing my words with his better-than-human hearing, but he didn't turn back and scold me.

"He has a lot on his mind," Bishop said as he gracefully sank to the ground beside me, slid his hand under the back of my shirt, and pressed his palm against my skin.

His touch reignited the fire in my core that I'd tried to get down to a manageable level with my morning orgasms.

"Not going to pull me into your lap," I breathed.

"If we want to leave in ten minutes, probably not a good idea," Bishop said, his voice strained. "But you still need as much contact as we can give you."

"You mean, *you*," I said around a mouthful of oatmeal flavored with chunks of last night's rabbit. "As much contact as *you* can give me."

"Cyrus will help if you need him." Bishop's attention jumped to his brother and his expression grew sad. "But he's got obligations to the pack and he's worried—"

"It's okay," I said, cutting him off, knowing he was going to bring up the fact that I was a powerless shifter and not worthy to be Cyrus's mate whether I wanted to be his mate or not. Right now, I was turned on and achy, not icy and hollow, and I wanted to keep it that way. "I understand."

I finished my breakfast and washed my bowl and the oatmeal pot while Bishop took the telescopic metal pieces making up the rotisserie, shrunk them down, and secured them in his pack.

Everyone grabbed their packs and we headed off again, this time leaving the road to wade through the thigh-high grass. My feet and legs started complaining right away but there wasn't anything I could do about it, so I tried to distract myself by looking at the stunning scenery of endless rolling foothills and, when we reached the top of a hill, the forests in the distance.

By mid-morning we crested the top of a tall hill and looked down at a thick, dark forest. Mist seeped from between the trunks and melted the second it reached the sunlight, and the weight of something dark and ominous whispered against my senses.

It felt like the power I sensed from the shifters around me, particularly Deacon and Cyrus who had so much power they struggled to contain it, except somehow I knew it wasn't coming from a shifter.

"Stay on the trail and stay by Bishop," Cyrus said, his attention locked on the forest. "There are beasts and spirits in Darkweald. Some more dangerous than grimalkins."

He didn't wait for me to answer before striding down

the hill toward a marginally wider opening among the trunks. Four brown wolves rushed down the hill ahead of him and slipped into the misty darkness. Deacon stayed with me, Bishop, and Whil, while Knox was already in the forest.

I hadn't seen him since the meeting in Whil's greenhouse cottage, but I could always sense him, and my attention kept jumping to wherever I felt he was even though I couldn't see him and didn't want to look for him.

The marginally wider opening among the trees was a narrow trail that forced us to walk in single file, leaving me feeling exposed on either side the second we crossed the threshold into the forest and were cloaked in shadows and mist and silence. There was no bird song or even the sound of leaves rustling in the wind.

The only sounds were our footsteps crunching on dead leaves and twigs, and the heavy ominous power seemed to muffle even that. It thankfully didn't grow in strength, but it was like it had substance and had plugged up my ears and nose.

"Do you have spirits in your realm?" Bishop whispered as if he didn't want to disturb the hush among the trees or perhaps grab the attention of whatever possessed the ominous dark power.

"I don't know. I've never seen or heard of one, but that doesn't mean they don't exist in my realm," I replied, although for all I knew his realms spirits were supers I already knew about and were called something else.

"They're manifestations of a god's power," he said.

"The closer you get to a god or goddess's resting place, the more likely you are to encounter one."

"How powerful are these manifestations?" I asked, peering into the thick, misty shadows around us. The guys had said there was a malicious god sleeping in this forest, which meant these spirits wouldn't be friendly.

"They get more powerful the closer you get to the god."

"And how close are we getting?" Although I had a bad feeling I already knew the answer.

Too close, Deacon said in my head. *To the heart of Anakar. But most of the area is out in the open, so we should be fine if we leave the forest before sundown.*

Which would explain why Cyrus didn't want to spend the night here... not that I'd want to spend the night even with just the pressure from the ominous power.

AUDREY

We continued in silence, everyone tense, including Cyrus, searching the shadows for danger. Power rolled off him as well as Bishop and Deacon, crackling against my senses, but thankfully not compelling me to do anything... well, maybe it was. I couldn't stop peering into the shadows as well, twitching every time I thought I heard or saw something. And oftentimes, that something was the rusty fur of one of the hunt team members who followed on either side of us, weaving between the trees and bushes.

I wasn't sure how long we walked before we reached a break in the trees. According to my feet and legs and back, it was all day, but it couldn't have been since Cyrus had said we'd reach Anakar by noon. Beyond, bathed in brilliant sunlight, was a large stone arch carved with images of people in agony, welcoming us to the partial ruins of a large town... or was it a temple complex?

The trail widened, becoming the remains of an old road paved with wide, flat stones, although at least half of the stones were missing or covered in layers of dirt and debris. Two dozen wide, shallow steps led up to a courtyard-type area with the crumbling remains of what once had been a large fountain with an enormous statue — now worn beyond recognition by the elements. It sat in the courtyard's center, surrounded by crumbling one- and two-story buildings, some no more than just a partial wall and the outline of where the other walls had stood.

Beyond that, towering above the remains of the buildings, was the temple, an intricate structure with dozens of spires and gaping black windows.

Deacon took the lead, taking us past the courtyard into a maze of narrow streets littered with rubble and forest debris. Mist curled among the stones where the sunlight couldn't reach and the dark power pressing against my senses grew stronger.

Then the maze opened up into a grander, bigger courtyard with a fountain and statue right in front of the temple. Unlike the statue in the previous fountain, this one was in good condition, clearly showing the monster that Sterling had summoned.

My pulse lurched as I looked up at the thing that had tried to eat me and *had* eaten Merrick while he was still alive.

Its leathery wings were spread wide, and his head, with its ram horns curling from his forehead, was tipped back, his mouth open. He had a person in each hand, their expressions filled with horror, and one hand was raised up to his mouth to devour the unfortunate soul.

That had almost been me.

And from what Sterling and Royce had said, they'd known that was going to be my fate. They really were psychopaths and I hoped to God that thing had eaten them as well. It would have served them right.

Four pillars, carved showing more people in pain, stood around the fountain marking a large square in the center of the courtyard, and between the two on my left, hanging in the air, was a tall shimmering thread.

"That's definitely magic," Whil said, heading toward the shimmering thread. Cyrus and Deacon followed her, stopping a good distance from whatever it was to examine it.

"Do you know what it is?" Cyrus asked.

"It's a rip in our realm," Whil replied, keeping her distance as well and slowly circling the *rip*.

Beyond the rip, the forest had taken over the buildings, crowding close to this one side of the courtyard.

I walked to the trees' edge and peered into the shadows. I couldn't see more than a few feet into the gloom, but when I closed my eyes and concentrated, I could hear the rushing of fast-moving water.

"It's the rip I came out of," I said, a confusing mix of hope and fear and frustration churning inside me.

"Does this mean Audrey can go home?" Bishop asked.

Did I want to go home?

No. I was happier here than I'd ever been back home.

But once the mating bond was broken and I was back to just being a powerless shifter would Bishop and Cyrus treat me like Sterling and Royce had? Would I want to return home then?

The rip's shimmering brightened and instead of just rippling air that distorted the statue beyond it — like the air over hot asphalt on a summer's day — a forest grove appeared, one that looked a lot like my old pack's sacred grove.

Now that I could get a good look at it, I could see that the window was tall, stretching taller than the statue but only a foot wide, and as I watched, a sparrow, chased by a crow, darted through the rip. The crow swooped after it, but one of its wings clipped the milky, shimmering edge of the rip and burst into flames, burning so hot and fast the bird was complete ash before it could hit the ground.

My churning emotions shifted to fear and, much to my surprise, disappointment. Maybe I did want to go home.

No, it wasn't going home that I wanted, but to show Bishop my realm. He'd been so interested in hearing about TV and I knew he'd be amazed to actually see it.

"She's not going home through that," Cyrus said, his voice gruff.

"Then how did she make it through?" Bishop asked.

"It was probably wider when it was first made," Whil replied. "But there's nothing maintaining it so the magic that created it is fading, and the rip is shrinking. Eventually, it'll disappear."

Cyrus gave Whil a nod and grunted then shielded his eyes and looked up. "We have a little time before we have to move out. Audrey, eat something. Bishop, you're with me and the hunt team. I want to search the area for trouble. Deacon, you're with Whil."

He jerked his chin and two of the wolves from the hunt team followed him across the courtyard and around the edge of the temple.

Bishop drew up close to me and slipped his hand under my shirt, pressing his palm against the small of my back.

My churning emotions eased and a flicker of that warmth and calm I'd felt last night replaced them.

"You okay?" he asked, his eyes soft and sad. "I know you weren't happy in your pack, but it's still home."

"There are things I wish I could show you, but I'd much rather be here than there." I shrugged and gave him my warmest smile. His eyes darkened and my body heated.

With a groan, he yanked his attention away and cleared his throat.

"You should eat and I should patrol," he said, then he marched away before I could respond.

I sat in the shade on a chunk of stone at the edge of a crumbled building, pulled out my bag of dried fruit and meat, and stared at the strip of green in the rip.

Whil walked around the rip a couple more times then, with Deacon at her side, headed to the temple. I wasn't sure what she was looking for, but I had to remember that her trip here wasn't about finding me a way home. It was about determining if the magic that had brought me here had awakened the malicious god and taken him to my realm.

From the dark, ominous power pressing against my senses, I suspected the god was still here, and from the fact that we hadn't been attacked or heard of attacks in the last few days since I'd come here, he was still asleep. But that didn't mean he wasn't close to waking up.

Fear shivered down my spine. Merrick, my old pack's alpha, hadn't stood a chance against that monster, and while Cyrus, Bishop, and Knox were all more powerful than Merrick, I had no idea if they'd be able to kill it.

Could someone even kill a god? Not to mention even if they did win, no one would get out of that kind of fight without injury, most likely life-changing injury.

AUDREY

I CHEWED ON A TOUGH PIECE OF DRIED MEAT AND WATCHED the leaves in the trees through the rip flutter in a breeze I couldn't feel. From the sunlight filtering through the branches, it looked to be about the same time of day there as it was here, and I could almost imagine I wasn't in a different realm.

Rustling sounded somewhere beyond where I could see, then Royce stepped into sight.

Instinct seized me and I froze as my pulse lurched into a desperate, rapid beat. He'd gleefully tried to sacrifice me to a monster. I had his claw marks scarring my chest, marks I'd never be able to get rid of even if my wolf did eventually awaken because they'd already healed. They were forever a part of my body, a reminder that he and Sterling were psychopaths.

And a part of my soul still wept at his rejection, still believed he was my destined mate, even though it had all been a manipulation and my soul had picked someone else.

Well, fuck that.

I tried to shove aside the unwanted grief as well as my fear and feed my anger.

What I felt was an after-effect of the spell he'd used to fake the fated mating call, nothing more, and that disgusting spell was why my soul thought Knox was my mate and why I'd forced a soul bond on him.

I wasn't in love with Royce and never would be. Just like I wasn't in love with Knox. And while Knox could still hurt me, and was hurting me by rejecting our unwanted bond, Royce couldn't touch me anymore. He couldn't get through the rip to get to me— Hell, he might not even be able to see through it like I could.

As if he could hear my thoughts, he glanced at the rip and looked straight at me. His eyes flashed wide for a second, revealing his surprise, then his lips curled back in a wicked smile.

"Well, look who's still alive," he sneered.

I stood and glared back. He couldn't get to me, but I refused to stay sitting and look up at him, even from a distance. Sitting was a weaker position and I wanted to make sure he knew he hadn't broken me and never would.

"How's your incomplete mating bond, *mate*?" he asked.

"It'll fade," I lied. I didn't want to bring Knox into this. For all I knew, he'd side with Royce about how useless I was and I wouldn't be able to fight the grief from our rejected bond. "Soon you'll be nothing more than a bad memory."

"You keep thinking that." His smile darkened with dangerous glee. "We got that witch to put extra juice into her spell. That feeling of emptiness, of utter rejection?" he said. "That feeling will never go away. It's just going to keep on growing until you lose your mind and kill yourself."

My breath stalled and I fought to keep the fear that was now rushing through me from my expression.

It was never going to go away?

But it had to. I couldn't spend the rest of my life feeling like this.

"That's a lie," I said, forcing myself to hide my fear and keep my voice strong.

"You're going to kill yourself just like Daddy." He jerked forward a step, and I flinched even though I *knew* he couldn't get to me.

He threw his head back and roared with laughter. "He ate a bullet in the bathtub."

And there'd been so much blood sprayed across the dated yellow tiles.

"How will you do it? Got a gun? Got pills?"

The grief and icy hollowness that I'd been trying so hard to ignore surged, consuming my anger, and my eyes started to burn with tears I did *not* want to cry in front of Royce.

No one wanted me—

Damn it. It isn't a real emotion.

Except it was and the rejected bond was just shining a spotlight on how I'd felt after finding my dad. I hadn't been enough for him to fight his PTSD from the war. I wasn't enough for anyone.

"Looks like you're going to have to find something sharp and slit your wrists." Something rustled out of my line of sight and he glanced over at whatever it was. "Look who's still kicking," he laughed.

Sterling stepped up beside him, his expression darker, although he still seemed pleased — in that same psychopathic sick way that Royce did — that I was still alive.

"Well, well, well," Sterling purred. "Are you broken yet?"

"Never," I spat back, blinking away my tears. I might be hurting, I might get beaten down and be a complete mess, but I refused to let Sterling and Royce break me. "And you can't get to me anymore."

His expression snapped to sudden, violent rage, and a ferocious wave of his power slammed into me.

"Come," he snarled.

My body jerked forward a step.

Oh, shit. He can control me through the rip.

I fought to step back, but all I managed to do was to stop myself from moving forward.

"I'm alpha and you're pack. You belong to me. Come," he growled.

No. No way in hell. Never.

"I'll always be able to get to you," he sneered.

His compulsion squeezed my chest and I stumbled forward a few more steps. I clenched every muscle in my body and glared at him. His power wasn't as strong as Cyrus's, and I'd managed to resist him... at least until I'd passed out. I wouldn't give in to Sterling. I wouldn't.

"I. Said. Come."

"Fuck you," I spat back even as his compulsion heaved me forward another step.

The wind on their side gusted, blowing a flurry of dead leaves at the rip, half of them flying through and half bursting into flames.

Sterling's eyes lit up with wicked glee. Forty more feet and that would be me.

No. Fuck no!

Something small and quiet *thu-thudded* around my heart, and I staggered back a step, shocking myself and — from the look on their faces — shocking Royce and Sterling as well.

Holy shit, I'd defied his command.

But his rage returned, wilder and darker than before, and his face turned red with the strength of his emotion. The ghostly image of ram's horns flickered around his head, curling from his forehead, and the dark, ominous power I'd been sensing since we'd entered the forest slammed into me and seized my muscles.

I staggered forward a step and then another and another, running full out toward the rip.

Oh shit. Oh shit oh shit oh shit.

I mentally clawed inside myself trying to find whatever power I had that had let me take a step back, but there was nothing inside me, no hint of a wolf or wisp of shifter power. I tried to fall, to let my body go limp, but Sterling's command was too strong, and my body wouldn't obey me.

Please. There had to be something I could do. I'd survived that monster — barely, but I'd survived — I couldn't go out like this.

Kneel! Knox yelled inside my head, and a massive wave of power crashed into me, seizing all my muscles and stealing my breath.

I dropped to my knees, gasping for air, the warring pressure from Sterling's power and Knox's making it difficult to breathe. Royce and Sterling dropped to the ground as well and Knox bounded out of the shadows of a crumbling house. He stopped beside me, growling and baring his teeth at the psychopaths.

"Found yourself a new alpha," Sterling snarled, defying Knox's power and heaving up to one knee. "He's not stronger than me."

He raised his hands and black things — shadows, demons, I had no idea what they were — exploded out of the ground in a stinging shower of stone and dirt.

They whirled around us, too many to count, their bodies twisting and expanding into flying snakes. They were all black, black scales, black leathery wings, and black teeth, so many black shark-like teeth. The only things not black were their glowing red eyes.

Sterling howled with laughter but abruptly stopped when the shimmering around the edge of the rip flickered brighter.

"Kill them," he snarled. "When the window reappears, I want to see their bodies torn to pieces."

The rip shimmered again, and Sterling, Royce, and my old pack's sacred grove vanished, the rip, once again, turning into a rippling thread of distorted air.

Then the snakes attacked in a writhing, hissing mass. One swooped at my head, I swatted it aside, and dropped to my knees, praying if I was on the ground, I'd be a smaller target.

Snarling, Knox caught a snake in midair with his teeth and, with a sickening crunch, bit it in half, then swiped his claws through two more. Another one sank its fangs into his back and I ripped it off, but that left me open, and two more bit my arm and back.

Screaming, I tried to wrench them off, but more snakes latched on and another wrapped around my throat.

AUDREY

I WRENCHED THE SNAKE FROM AROUND MY NECK BEFORE IT could strangle me, panic making me slam it against the ground again and again until its strange, glowing red blood had splattered me, Knox, and the ground.

My breath sawed in my chest from exertion and fear, and I had no idea how we were going to survive this or even just escape.

"What the fuck?" Cyrus roared, suddenly right beside me.

He yanked the snakes off me then swiped his claws through three more, splattering me with more blood.

I wrenched another snake off Knox and bashed it against a snake on the ground, killing both of them. My back, arms, and legs stung where they'd bitten me, and while the snakes weren't enormous, they weren't small either, and my arms were starting to get tired from all the swatting and yanking and swinging.

"How many are there?" Bishop asked, rushing up to us and boxing me in between the three of them.

"No, fucking clue," Cyrus growled. "I've killed at least a dozen but it doesn't look like I've made a dent."

Someone howled, and I glanced through the writhing swarm. Three of the four hunt team members were halfway between us and the temple, biting and clawing at snakes, while the fourth lay on the ground. Blood — our colored blood, not the snakes — rushed around her, and I jerked to my feet.

I couldn't really fight, but maybe I could do something to save her.

"Stay," Cyrus barked, his command slamming into me before I could go.

"She'll die."

"You'll die and my brother will be fucked," he snarled back as a snake on the ground shot out and dug its fangs into his calf.

I stomped on the snake with a stomach-churning crunch. "Your brother will be free."

"You don't know that," he said, tearing through two more.

Across the courtyard, Deacon and Whil bolted out of the temple followed by more snakes. She shot a golf ball-sized blast of golden light at a snake, and it fell to the ground, but two more took its place.

There are too many, Cyrus said in my head. *Deacon, you and your team get Whil out of the forest.*

"I haven't finished my investigation," she yelled back

as she and Deacon reached the three remaining hunt team members, and they all fought their way closer to us.

Send a hunt team in to investigate before you come back and don't return without at least two teams.

"And when the window is open, don't let anyone from my realm see you," I said, stomping on another snake.

Cyrus shot me a dark look that said once we were safe he was getting answers whether he had to compel them out of me or not.

Deacon, you, Nova, and Finn decide if the town can spare two teams, Cyrus added, slashing a snake out of the air just before it bit me. *If not, don't come back. Knox, get Audrey out of here.*

Get on my back, Knox said, surprising me that he'd allow me to touch him let alone ride him. He was big, bigger than all the wolves in my old pack, almost the size of a pony, but still—

"I'm too heavy. I'll slow you down," I said. "I can run."

Get. On. My. Back. His command seized me and I scrambled onto his back before I could stop myself.

"Stop commanding me." His power made me lean over him and grab fistfuls of fur, enveloping me in his rich smoky scent.

Then do what I say when I say it. He leaped forward, his muscles bunching underneath me, his movement smooth and powerful as if he wasn't carrying me.

He barreled through the snake swarm, past the crumbling buildings, and into the forest. The snakes flew after us, hissing and snapping. One bit my thigh, but Knox bashed us against a tree, knocking the thing off and sending throbbing pain through my leg.

He leaped and wove his way through the trees and underbrush. Leaves and branches sliced at my cheeks, and I buried my face against his neck to protect it, fully wrapping myself in his scent.

Home. He was where I belonged. We were meant to be together. Always.

I struggled to concentrate beyond the warmth in my soul at our physical contact and the heat between my thighs at the knowledge that I was straddling him. It didn't matter that he was in his wolf form at the moment. He could shift into a man and be completely naked and ready in an instant.

Behind us, Cyrus and Bishop crashed through the underbrush, racing after us in their human forms, but they weren't fast enough to keep up and Knox quickly outpaced them, awakening a gnawing worry within me.

There were just the two of them and there were so many snakes, and I didn't know if they'd be able to outrun them. Of course, they could sacrifice their clothes and shift, but that thought didn't make the worry disappear.

"We have to go back for them," I said, tightening my grip in his fur as if that would alert him to how much we had to go back. "We can't leave them behind."

They can take care of themselves, he said, not slowing. *You can't.*

"Knox, please."

No.

"Knox—" Damn it. I hated that he was right. I could jump off and run back to Cyrus and Bishop, but I wouldn't be any help, and that was only if I could find them. And only if Knox didn't command me back onto him.

"They're your brothers."

He didn't reply, just kept running. The hiss and rush of air from the swarming snakes died off, but he didn't slow or hesitate until we crashed out of the underbrush onto a trail similar to the one we'd taken into the forest.

My emotions churned, a complicated hot mess that I just couldn't seem to control. My body screamed at me to have sex with Knox, now now now, but I also felt warm and safe and comfortable just like I had when Bishop had held me, while my stomach was heavy and aching with worry for Bishop and Cyrus along with the fear that Sterling and Royce would be able to reach me even now.

And on top of all of that, I was angry.

Angry that I couldn't escape those psychopaths, that I'd been wrong about being safe on this side of the rip, and that I'd been useless in that fight.

Knox rounded a curve in the trail and slowed down to a fast walk. Up ahead lay the way out, a brilliant opening, framed by the forest's dense, dark branches and mist.

What the hell were you thinking talking to them? Knox demanded, finally deciding to speak to me again as we crossed the threshold into the too-bright light of late afternoon.

I'd been thinking that I wanted to prove to Sterling that even if I didn't have any power, I was strong and a survivor. I'd never fought back before. I'd always kept out of sight as best I could and taken what he'd given when he found me. I'd thought for once I was safe and I could tell him how I really felt.

Boy, had I been wrong.

And jeez, I can't believe you thought that asshole was your mate, Knox added, his mental voice thick with disgust, as if everything was my fault because I was too stupid to know the truth.

"Don't you dare!" I shoved off his back, stumbled, my sore legs unsteady, then found my balance and glared at him.

His dark eyes captured mine and my soul wept that we'd lost physical contact while my body flip-flopped between empty and cold, achy and hot, and angry.

"They're the ones who manipulated me. They enspelled me. I'm sorry the magic they used on me forced us into a mating bond, but don't you dare blame me for what happened." I wasn't stupid. I'd just been hopeful. So God damned, foolishly hopeful.

Royce had made me believe that there was someone out there who could love me, made me think I was worth loving. That, more than anything, was the cruelest thing he and Sterling had done to me. I hadn't realized how much I'd suppressed my hope, or how much hope I'd still had.

Shame and anger burned over my cheeks and forehead. In a matter of minutes, he'd given me everything I hadn't even known I'd been praying for.

It had happened too fast for me to fully process what was going on. I'd only known that a spark I'd kept hidden had suddenly burst into a flame and I wanted what the fated mating call promised.

Then he'd ripped it all away.

I'm not blaming you, Knox said, his voice still harsh and angry. *It's just obvious he isn't your type.*

"Oh, and you know my type?" I shot back. Not that I'd been given a choice. No one had been interested in me and the magic they'd used had convinced me we'd been fated for each other. "You've barely spoken to me, you want nothing to do with me, but you know my type?" Understanding hit me like a punch to the gut. "Right. He's powerful. Someone like me could never be with someone powerful like him."

Actually, I hadn't thought you were into assholes. He turned away, looking across the rugged, rocky landscape ahead of us clearly ending our conversation.

I glared at him as if I could will him into feeling all the frustration and turmoil and heartache I felt. I wanted to scream, fight, bash more snakes on the ground, something, anything to relieve the pressure building inside me. My insides twisted and everything felt too tight and too hot and too much.

I jerked a few steps toward the forest, needing to take action, even if it was just moving.

You're waiting here, Knox snarled.

"I know that," I snapped back, heaving myself around and marching away from him.

And you're not going far. A hint of his power fluttered over me and I ground my teeth, refusing to submit.

I stomped back toward the forest, getting a few steps farther before he growled at me, then marched away again.

Do something. Do something, my mind hissed at me over and over again. *Be useful.*

I raked my gaze around me, searching for something to prove my usefulness. Great chunks of rock jutted from a sloping, jagged landscape covered with moss and dense bushes, and in the distance were more forests. It looked more like we were higher up the mountains than lower and the only explanation for that was that Cyrus's pack's town wasn't in the foothills but a valley.

Except I hadn't seen any mountains on the horizon, which only reminded me that my realm's logic didn't necessarily apply here. And while I would guess that the river cutting through Darkweald Forest flowed through these rocks, I couldn't assume it was. Not to mention all this rock could have made it turn away from its north-south direction before we'd even left Darkweald.

Fine. I couldn't fill our canteens. Not that I'd be able to know if the water was safe. And while I could gather twigs from the nearby bushes, they wouldn't be nearly enough for a fire — and I doubted Knox would even let me go to the forest's edge to gather wood. I also couldn't tell if there were any good spots around for us to camp.

Again, not that we'd stay this close to the forest and those snakes.

I turned back to Knox. A small pool of blood lay on the ground by his back paw and even though his fur was black, I could still see the sticky gloss of blood on his upper back thigh, shoulder, and snout.

Damn it. I'd forgotten my pack back at the ruins and I didn't even have supplies for first aid. Of course, given that he wasn't seriously bleeding, he could easily shift and heal himself which meant even if I had our supplies, I'd still be useless... and he'd be naked.

Oh, God.

I wrenched away from him again, making him growl.

For the love of— Stop. Pacing. His command jerked me to a stop. *I'm trying to listen for them.*

I sagged to the ground and closed my eyes. If I couldn't do anything and wasn't permitted to pace, I might as well listen, too. Not that my hearing was as good as Knox's, but it gave me something to focus on.

AUDREY

A MOMENT LATER KNOX HUFFED AND THE TENSION IN HIS body eased, relaxing some of the churning worry inside me. I hadn't heard Cyrus or Bishop, but somehow I knew Knox had. It still didn't mean they were okay, but if he was relaxing, it meant both of them were still moving and that was a good sign.

A few minutes later, I heard their footsteps on the hardpacked earth of the trail and opened my eyes to watch them jog out of the gloomy forest into the afternoon sunlight.

Their shirts and pants were bloodstained and ripped, and Bishop's cheek was bleeding, the blood running down his neck and into his shirt, but neither of them were limping or holding themselves as if they were seriously injured.

I rushed to meet Bishop and tried to pull his pack from his shoulders. "You need to shift."

"He can wait until we're farther away," Cyrus said. His expression was hard, and he looked fiercer than normal with a wide streak of blood painted across his right cheek. "Can you wait on first aid as well?"

"Yes." From the bloodstain on my still-throbbing thigh — that was definitely bruised from being bashed against a tree — and on my ripped shirt, I knew I was bleeding, but I wasn't bleeding a lot. I also wasn't light-headed, confirming that even though they stung, they weren't bad, which surprised me. I had no idea how I'd managed to get through that fight more or less unscathed.

"Good." He shoved my pack at me and glared. "Forget it again and it's gone. I won't pick it up a second time."

"Understood," I said, unable to stop myself from shrinking a step away from him.

Cyrus huffed and turned his glare to the sky. "We've got at least five hours until sunset. Knox, find fresh water so Audrey can quickly clean up and we can check her injuries before carrying on."

Bishop shot Cyrus a look.

"No." Cyrus strode away, their argument over before it had even begun, and followed the only path available that might or might not have been a continuation of the trail from the forest. "Want to tell me what happened back in the ruins?" he asked me.

Not really.

But there was no point in refusing to talk or lying. Cyrus would just force me to tell him everything or Knox would fill him in — because I had no doubt Knox had seen and heard everything.

"The men who tried to sacrifice me appeared on the other side of the rip. Apparently, alpha powers work through it and he wasn't happy I was still alive."

The memory of Sterling's power and the ghostly image of the malicious god's horns sprouting from his forehead shuddered through me.

"I hope Whil and the others are careful or the rip closes soon," I added. "I think Sterling got the power he wanted. When Knox stopped him from making me walk into the rip, he summoned those flying snakes."

"You think he'd attack the others even if you're not around?" Bishop asked.

"I think he's a psychopath who just got more powerful," I replied.

Bishop brushed his hand against my lower back and offered me a soft smile that I was sure was supposed to be reassuring and supportive but actually reminded me that I ached to have sex with him.

I tried to smile back without looking like I wanted to tear his clothes off and jump him then hurried after Cyrus.

Ahead, the path led down a steep slope and I couldn't tell if steps had been cut into it or not. There were enough places to step that I wouldn't skid all the way to the bottom on my ass, but that was only if I was careful since some of the *steps* were barely larger than my foot.

Below and beyond a thicket of scraggly shrubs lay the

river, its water sparkling in the sunshine, and as much as I had said I was fine to carry on, I was grateful that I wouldn't have to go far before washing the snake blood off my face, hands, and arms. That, and I was starting to feel my aching legs and feet, along with every stinging bite from the snakes.

Maybe I wasn't so fine after all, and I'd only thought I was because of adrenaline.

Knox sat just before the thicket waiting for us. He was still in his wolf form, but his fur was no longer glossy and matted with blood, indicating that he'd shifted out his injuries while he'd waited for us to join him, which meant he'd been in his human form and naked.

That thought turned the sexual ache from Bishop's smile into a need as strong as the need I'd felt after I had one of my sexy dreams. It didn't matter that I hurt and was bleeding and filthy. My need to seal the bond, to have sex, to ease the pressure building between my thighs was suddenly overwhelming.

Damn it. I didn't want that. I wanted to break our mate bond. But if Bishop and Cyrus were going to shift out their injuries, they'd need to be naked too, and that—

My breath picked up and I tried to clamp down on that thought. Except I couldn't stop thinking about the one time I'd seen Cyrus naked. He'd been streaked with blood from fighting the grimalkins, and that had only made him look more ferocious and dangerous and incredibly sexy. He was all powerful muscle, honed from years of training and fighting, and his cock—

I was pretty sure I'd only seen it at half mast, but it had still been impressive. More impressive than Sterling at full mast when I'd accidentally walked in on him in the bathroom, something I wished I could bleach from my memory.

"Bishop." Cyrus jerked his chin toward the river, the muscles in his jaw tightening as if he knew what I was thinking — and while he didn't know the details, I had no doubt he could smell my arousal and knew I was thinking about sex. "Help Audrey."

My pulse picked up at the double meaning of his words.

"Come on." Bishop hopped down a three-foot ledge and held out his hand to help me.

I stared at it, afraid of what would happen if I touched him, afraid of how I wanted to throw myself into his arms and beg him to release the pressure.

He'd said he'd have sex with me if I needed it.

Did I need it?

Or did I just want it?

Did it matter?

Embarrassment burned my cheeks. Sex with Bishop complicated things, and having sex with him didn't mean he'd give me the thing I really wanted: someone to care about me. I didn't know if I'd be able to have casual sex with him and not have my heartbroken. And did I really want my first time to be out in the middle of nowhere, with his brothers listening while I was sore and tired and covered in sticky snake blood?

AUDREY

Bishop grabbed my hand, sending a shock of need snapping up my arm and shooting straight to my core.

My breath hitched and I dropped my gaze to my feet, afraid to look him in the eyes, as he tugged me forward, forcing me to hop down closer to him. Heat radiated from him, caressing my senses, urging me to lean into him, take comfort in his touch and in his body.

"I don't want to do something stupid," I murmured as he led me around the thicket and down to the river's rocky shallows.

"But you think you're going to?" he asked, his voice just as soft, although I was sure Cyrus and Knox could still hear us with their better-than-human hearing.

"I think I'm going to lose my mind and we've only just started this journey." I set my pack on the bank, sagged at the water's edge, and started scrubbing the snake blood off my hands. "I'm in no condition for anything and yet it's all I can think about. Hell, we just got attacked by flying snake things. I should be freaking out or something. And if we can't break the bond with Knox, then losing control now could make a bad situation worse." And now I was just babbling.

"Knox will understand," he said, kneeling on the ground beside me and washing his hands as well. He was close, but not as close as I wanted, and yet not far enough away.

"You say that but—" I splashed water on my face, cleaning away the blood.

"No buts," he said when I came up for air, and he hook his finger under my chin, drawing my gaze up to his.

I fell into his warm brown eyes, every part of me, body, heart, and soul, mesmerized by the bright green flecks in his irises. He was so beautiful and kind, and the warmth I'd felt when he'd held me last night had to mean we had some kind of a connection. Only a mate, family member, or very close friend could affect a shifter's soul like that, and he was neither a family member nor a close friend.

"Strong heats can require more than one partner to get through," he said, drawing my attention to his lips and making me wonder how they would feel against mine. "Even if you were happily mated, he'd understand if you needed extra help."

"But you didn't kiss me before," I breathed, leaning toward him, unable to help myself. We'd almost kissed twice now and every time he'd backed away. He had to have a reason for not kissing me and I doubted those reasons had changed.

"You weren't in heat." Now it was his turn for his gaze to flicker to my lips, and his wolf darkened his eyes with an intense desire that stole my breath. "Or at least, we didn't know you were in heat."

Right. My heat. And once it was over, his reasons would return. He'd told me yesterday he'd have sex with me with no expectations. I'd thought he'd meant it to reassure me that he wouldn't want a commitment if I didn't want one, but now I was sure it had been to warn me. We could have sex, but I shouldn't expect it to mean anything.

Sure, the look in his eyes right now said he wanted me, but I was releasing pheromones like crazy. Once my heat was over, I'd no longer be influencing him and he'd no longer desire me.

And right now, my body didn't care.

Hell, none of me cared. I *needed* relief. I was going to lose my mind and he was looking at me like I was desirable even though my clothes were ripped and bloody.

I closed the distance between us before I could second guess myself and pressed my lips against his. He stiffened and the fear that I'd misread the situation twisted in my gut.

Then he groaned softly and cupped the back of my head, gently holding me in place. This kiss was the complete opposite to my dreams where Knox had ferociously dominated me, pulling my hair and devouring my mouth as if he were starving. Bishop's kiss was tender, reverent.

His tongue teased the seam between my lips, asking permission, and his grip remained soft as if he were waiting for me to come to my senses and pull away. But my senses had vanished the second I'd thought of all three of them shifting into their naked human form, and now the heat in my core was lava.

I opened my lips to him, slipping my tongue into his mouth first, urging him for more.

A rumble rolled out of his throat and he kissed me harder, raking his tongue against mine and devouring my gasp of pleasure as his free hand pushed under my shirt and stroked a searing path up my ribs to my breasts.

My nipples were already tight, my breasts aching, and I arched into his touch no longer upset that this realm didn't seem to have bras... although now I was regretting not wearing that easy-to-slip-off dress. I could have been naked in an instant and wouldn't have had to worry about the awkwardness of trying to get my pants off.

The thought sent a flurry of nerves fluttering in my stomach. I was really going to have sex. Here. Now. I—

"Bishop," I gasped into his mouth. "I want—" He sucked on my bottom lip and his hand on my breasts dipped to the waistband of my pants. "But I've never—"

He stilled and my nerves froze into fear. Would he stop because I was a virgin?

Shit. I shouldn't have said anything.

"It's nothing. I—" I tried to press my lips back to his, but his hand that had been at my waist, slipped back up to my chest and gently held me back.

"No, it's something," he said, his voice husky. "Audrey, have you never had sex?"

The word sex shuddered through me. "I still need it."

He cupped my cheek with his large palm, his hunger softening a little.

"Please, don't make me beg," I implored, knowing how desperate I already sounded.

"I won't. I promise." His fingers dipped back down to my pants. "But I want you to enjoy it, so we need to go slow." He flicked the button on my fly. "And we don't have the time for slow right now, so—"

I opened my mouth to argue with him even though I knew Cyrus wasn't going to let us stay here long, but he pushed his hand down the front of my pants, and everything I'd just been thinking vanished.

"I'll relieve the pressure for now and we'll revisit this when we have time," he purred as his fingers teased through my curls and into my arousal.

I nodded, unable to form coherent words, and my hips rocked forward, my body knowing what it wanted even though all my experience had been in my dreams and with my own hands.

"Fuck, you're so wet," he groaned.

He swept his fingers across my entrance to my clit, and my inner muscles trembled. I'd been on the edge since I'd woken up this morning— Hell, I'd been on the edge for days and it wasn't going to take Bishop much to make me come.

Embarrassment heated my cheeks. I didn't want to come the second he touched me, but, God damn it, I was already so close.

He captured my lips again and teased his finger over my clit, twisting the achy, searing need inside me tighter and tighter. My breath turned ragged and my body trembled. I clung to him, my fingers digging into his shoulders, my forehead pressed against his, and then every muscle in my body contracted and stars flashed behind my lids.

A strangled sob escaped my lips, filled with relief and embarrassment and grief. It had happened so fast and wasn't as powerful as the one from my dreams. I wanted more. I wanted the fantasy. But this was reality and, if I was being honest with myself, the orgasm had still been a lot better than if I'd done it myself, even if it hadn't completely satisfied my body's craving.

Still shuddering, I collapsed against him. The warmth of our physical contact swelled around my heart, melting some of my embarrassment and grief.

He wrapped his arms around me and I nuzzled my face into the hollow of his neck, breathing in his fresh green scent. This was where I belonged, where I was safest. I was home.

Except I wasn't home.

Once this was over, all of this would be gone.

And I had to keep thinking like that. I couldn't afford to hope. I wouldn't survive my hope being shattered again. Not by Bishop. Because it was far too easy to fall in love with him.

BISHOP

I CLUNG TO AUDREY, MY WOLF HEAVING INSIDE ME, fighting to break free. She needed more than a quick release, and my throbbing cock was more than ready to give it to her. But I refused to let him take over. We didn't have the time to do it right, and I sure as hell was going to do it right.

Calm the fuck down. She's a virgin, I snarled at my wolf.

But he didn't understand what that meant. He was a primal force, and the scent of her arousal was working him into a frenzy that I wasn't sure I'd be able to control for much longer.

We needed to protect her and that included relieving the pressure from her heat. He didn't understand that we couldn't just push our cock into her and make her scream with pleasure. He didn't understand that she needed to be wet and relaxed and feeling safe so her first time wouldn't hurt. And while her heat would help a lot in the wet department, I didn't want to risk it not being enough. My wolf didn't understand any of that. He wanted her now now now because she needed us now now now.

"Bishop," Cyrus said, his voice low, making Audrey tense against me, probably not realizing that wasn't his angry voice but his stressed-out voice... or suddenly realizing that Cyrus and Knox had heard all her strained gasps and her confusing sob when she'd come. "We need to get farther away from Darkweald."

"I ah—" She sucked in a ragged breath. "I think I should clean myself up... alone."

"You won't be able to patch yourself up by yourself," I replied, letting her push away from me. Her cheeks were red with embarrassment even though her expression was still hungry with desire.

"If you touch me—" Her gaze slid down my body to where I tented my pants, and her expression grew pained. "Cyrus should do it."

Do it? My thoughts instantly jumped to sex and my wolf snarled. I was here. I could take care of her. She didn't need my brother.

Except that wasn't what she was saying. She didn't think she'd be able to hold it together while I helped her, and we both knew we needed to keep moving. Even if those flying snakes didn't come out of the forest and we were safe from the malicious god's spirits, we still had to get to the death god's temple as soon as possible. And stopping for sex right now wouldn't help us. That, and I suspected from her sob that she had a lot of conflicting and confusing emotions around the whole situation.

"Okay." I forced myself to stand and climb back onto the bank. Cyrus had made it clear that he had no intention of sleeping with her and she probably sensed that in how he'd been keeping his distance from her.

I rounded the thicket where Cyrus and Knox waited. Cyrus's clothes were still ripped and bloody, but the streak of blood on his face was gone which meant he'd shifted out his injuries while he'd listened to me make her come.

I'm not sleeping with her, he said in my head.

Pretty sure that's why she asked for you.

He huffed and pushed past me, hopping off the bank onto the stream's rocky shallows.

"Get your clothes off and let me see," he growled, a hint of his power rolling off him.

Audrey stiffened and glared at him, the desire in her eyes shifting to frustration — which was probably Cyrus's intent.

"You don't have to make me," she snapped back, grabbing the bottom of her shirt and pulling it up over her head.

I turned away, sucking in deep breaths scented with her arousal that did nothing to ease my wolf or my raging hard-on.

Fuck. I needed to take care of that before I shifted out my injuries. If I couldn't get myself back under control, my wolf really would take over when I shifted and take us right back to her.

"Call me when they're done," I said to Knox, and marched farther away, trying to escape her scent. But it was on me, on my fingers, and clinging to my clothes, and I was going to have to figure out how to keep myself together while holding her this evening when we stopped for the night. Because as much as she probably needed a little sex, she still needed a lot of holding.

I yanked off my ruined shirt and shucked my pants. My cock jutted from my body, throbbing and hard and already leaking pre-cum, and with a groan, I gripped it tight in my fist.

I'd wanted so desperately to do more than just finger her. But I'd promised I wouldn't take advantage of her and a quick fuck when she'd never had sex before wasn't taking care of her. She deserved to be spread out on a soft bed, caressed, and gently teased until she was so wet and relaxed it wouldn't hurt at all.

I closed my eyes and the image of her on my bed in the Residence jumped into my mind. Her blond hair was splayed on the pillow behind her and her head was tipped back in pleasure offering me perfect access to her neck and the top of her shoulder.

My breath picked up and my canines extended in anticipation of claiming her even though this was a fantasy. I slid my hand to my tip, rubbing my palm over my pre-cum for lubrication, then pumped it back down.

I'd take my time with her, worship her, caressing and kissing my way down her body, and make her come before I even reached her sex. Her heat and inexperience made her hypersensitive, and I was going to take full advantage of that.

At the river, I'd barely gotten started with my fingers when she'd gasped and shuddered against me. I'd use that to bring her the most incredible pleasure over and over again with fingers, lips, and tongue, and then, once she was gasping and boneless and glowing, I'd slowly sink inside her.

I tightened my grip, working my hand faster up and down my length. She'd make those incredible sounds I'd overheard the other day when I'd been outside her bedroom, soft mewls and throaty groans and sharp gasps.

My balls tightened at the thought. Then she'd make that long shuddering moan— or better yet, she'd cry out my name like she cried out Knox's name in my dreams. Her body would light up with pleasure, our bond would light up with certainty, and—

Fuck.

My cock swelled and I shot cum onto the rocky ground in front of me. I clenched my jaw, fighting to swallow my own shuddering moan, and sagged back against the rock behind me to stay standing.

Fuck fuck fuck.

We didn't have a bond and I shouldn't be thinking like that until things were figured out between her and Knox. She had more than enough to worry about, and my wolf wanting to mate with her even though we barely knew each other could scare her away.

Hell, it was kind of scaring me away. Did I really want her as a mate or was that Knox's bond influencing me through our twin bond? And I wouldn't know the truth until they broke their bond or sealed it.

CYRUS

Bishop groaned, the sound just at the edge of my hearing, and my balls tightened in sympathy. Audrey's gasps and moans still rang in my ears, and the scent of her release hung heavy in the air around us. It was torture coming closer to her, forcing her to strip, and I could only imagine how much harder it was for Bishop actually having touched her.

Fuck me. I am not *sleeping with her. Not here. Not now. Not ever.*

And I sure as hell wasn't going to have a one-night stand with her. She deserved better than that.

She deserved the promise of forever.

But even if Bishop joined our mate bond, the pack still wouldn't accept her as an alpha, and I wasn't going to put her through that. No matter how much my wolf wanted her. She deserved to be worshiped and adored, valued for who she was not for how much power she possessed. Putting her in the public eye would only point out her weakness, and I feared she'd emotionally crumble and never recover from that.

She was already on the precipice. She might have glared at me for using my powers to make her strip, but even as she pulled off her boots and stepped out of her pants, she was shrinking in on herself. It was like watching a flower wilt before my eyes.

Now she crouched on the riverbank, her shoulders hunched, as she clutched her bloody shirt to her body, covering her breasts and groin as if she were ashamed.

Which made my wolf furious. Being naked was a natural part of being a shifter. If we didn't want to constantly be buying new clothes, we had to strip if we wanted to shift, and she had no reason to hide herself. It wasn't natural.

But that was just a reminder that *she* wasn't natural. Her pack had cursed themselves, preventing them from shifting until they were adults. She hadn't grown up with the casual nudity I had, and without a wolf form, she'd never needed to take her clothes off in front of anyone.

"Drop the shirt," I said, trying to keep my voice even and not reveal how much I was fighting to keep my wolf from wrapping our arms around her and comforting her. "It's only going to get in the way. I've seen it all already anyway," I added, hoping to relax her.

But she stiffened and turned red instead.

"That doesn't make me feel better," she murmured, dropping the shirt and thankfully not forcing me to make her. "Just hurry this up. I'm cold and—" A shiver rolled down her body from her head to her perfectly curved ass and her desire thickened around her. "And I'm pretty sure I'm not downwind from you."

No. No, you're not.

I bit back a rumble of desire and wrenched my gaze away from her to pull my first-aid kit from my pack. "You have a cloth in your pack. Wipe yourself down and let's see what we've got."

I heard her rummage in her pack and then the splash of water and turned to watch her slide the damp fabric over her shoulder and down her arm.

My wolf's focus snapped to her movement and the beads of water gathering on her skin. From this angle, I could see the swell of her breast, but her arm hid her nipple—

And now I was imagining the water beading on that dusky bud and my tongue licking it away.

Fuck me.

She had a couple of bites on her arm, as well as on her back, and I focused on those, reminding my wolf that while we wanted to claim her — which we sure as hell couldn't — she was still hurt and our first priority was to take care of her. We needed to assess her injuries, decide if she needed an elixir, and patch her up.

Surprisingly, she wasn't that hurt. She had a couple of nasty bites that Nova probably would have stitched up to be on the safe side since she healed like a human, a lot of cuts and scratches, and an enormous bruise blossoming over her right thigh, but nothing that seemed serious enough to warrant giving her one of our precious elixirs.

I patched her up as quickly as I could, trying to keep my touch professional and my expression distant, but by the time I'd taped on the last piece of gauze, her breath had picked up, her eyes dilated with desire, and her arousal thickened the air.

"We'll stop early tonight so Bishop can help you," I said, wrenching away from her to shove my first-aid kit back into my pouch.

Fuck, my cock hurt. I was hard from hearing her come and had only gotten harder as I'd patched her up. Touching and smelling her and knowing I was the one arousing her was pure torture. It didn't matter that her desire for me came from her heat and her incomplete mating bond and not from a genuine interest. My body and my wolf didn't care.

I needed to put some distance between us and she needed a good long fuck.

"I ah..." I heard her rummage through her pack again but refused to look at her. "Don't stop early."

I clenched my teeth, determined to not watch her get dressed. "You pretty much passed out the minute we stopped yesterday and today you're going to be even more tired."

"Good."

"Not good." My willpower cracked, and I glanced at her, grateful that she'd managed to put on the clean pair of pants that had been in her pack and was pulling down her shirt, hiding her breasts. "If your heat is affecting you this much, you're going to have to have sex. Cuddling with Bishop won't be enough. The sooner you deal with it, the sooner you'll be thinking straight."

"Cyrus, please." She pressed her hands against her chest, the motion she'd done last night when she'd felt Bishop's soul steadying hers. "I need this bond broken. My emotions are a mess, and if Bishop and I... It'll just get worse." Her cheeks flushed and she dropped her gaze to her feet. "What happened was a mistake. I can't— I'll —" She sucked in a deep breath, squared her shoulders, and met my gaze head-on again. Determination filled her expression even though her pupils were still blown out with desire. "No stopping early or starting late and no unnecessary breaks. I can push through. I *will* push through. I have to."

She was holding herself together on sheer will alone. I hadn't fully understood what she was going through with Knox rejecting their bond, hadn't thought she'd been experiencing the full effects so soon, but I could see the truth now. She'd been worn down to fragile glass in a matter of days and anything — like fearing Bishop would reject her once her heat was over — would shatter her. It wouldn't matter if I told her my brother was smitten with her. She didn't believe she had any value and couldn't imagine that someone would want to be with her.

And even if she could get past that, having sex with Bishop and knowing she'd never have it with her bonded mate — even if she didn't want that mate — could shatter her as well.

Fuck.

She was in a precarious position until the bond was broken. She probably didn't even know which emotions were really hers, which were the incomplete bond, and which were her heat.

"Fine," I forced out, my wolf angry that letting her suffer was the best solution to the problem.

I grabbed my pack and hopped up the bank, listening as she scrambled to follow. My cock throbbed and my wolf heaved inside me. Fuck I hated this. I hated that my wolf had finally become interested in someone and I couldn't have her, and I hated that I was going to make her suffer even if it was at her own damned request.

Bishop, I snarled. *Did you hear any of that?*

Yeah, he replied, his mental voice solemn. *I'll carry her if she starts to slow down.*

You both know she won't want that, Knox replied as he bounded up the rocks. *She needs to prove how strong she is. To you and to herself.*

"And here I thought he wasn't paying any attention," Bishop muttered as he climbed up after him.

I can still hear you, asshole, he huffed. *Anyone who spends two seconds with her can figure her out. One look at her face and you know exactly what she's feeling.*

That just makes you the asshole, Bishop replied. *You're breaking her soul and endangering her life on the slim chance that we'll be able to break the mating bond at the death god's temple.*

Pretty sure being stuck with me for life is worse, Knox shot back as he raced out of sight.

Did he just...? Bishop asked me.

The effects of a mating bond goes both ways, I replied and while that comment meant Knox was softening up to his unwanted mate, it also meant he was determined to not keep her. Just like Audrey, Knox struggled with seeing himself for who he truly was.

AUDREY

We hiked until I was sure I couldn't hike anymore and then hiked even farther. The sun sat low on the horizon when Cyrus finally stopped us for the night. My feet, legs, and back— hell, my whole body ached. The bruise on my thigh throbbed with every step, and the bite on my back stung, my backpack rubbing against it with each uneven step.

We'd stopped in an alcove, partially covered with a rocky overhang and sheltered from the wind on three sides. Our campsite sat at the edge of the woods that I'd seen far off in the distance and about sixty feet — and down a rocky incline — to the river.

Cyrus dropped his pack and tossed his and Knox's canteens to Bishop. "Fill those and set up camp. I'll get firewood."

"What can I do?" I asked, letting my pack fall to the ground. I was exhausted, just like I'd asked for, but if I didn't sit, I could probably help with something before I collapsed.

"Stay awake until dinner is done," Cyrus commanded and he marched toward the forest.

"It'll be easier with a job," I sighed, and Bishop offered me a sympathetic smile.

"Come on." He jerked his chin and I followed him down to the river. "Now take your boots off and soak your feet. According to the map, we've still got seven days until we reach the death god's territory and if we keep up this pace you're only going to feel worse."

"I'll feel worse if the bond forces me and Knox to seal it," I replied, sitting downstream from Bishop and pulling off my boots. "I think I can last seven days. Surely my heat will end soon. But I'm not sure if I can last longer."

"I've already promised that I won't let you do something you don't want to," Bishop reassured me.

I sank my feet into the cool water as he submerged the first canteen. "It's not just me fighting it. Wolves in my realm can be aggressive when it comes to their mate and the magic of this bond is..."

I shuddered, fighting my arousal, determined to stay in control. Except it was so much harder now that I knew what Bishop's lips felt like against mine, his hands caressing—

I clamped down on those thoughts and cleared my throat.

"The bond's magic is powerful. If it overwhelms Knox, he could hurt anyone who gets in his way," I finished.

Bishop closed the cap on the first canteen and started filling the second one. "Both of you are stubborn enough to resist it."

"I'd rather not press our luck any longer than we have to." My gaze flickered to Bishop's, but I managed to pull it away before I could fall into his warm, brown eyes.

"I understand," he replied, his voice husky. "You won't have to."

He filled the last canteen and then returned to camp, letting me soak my feet while he started to set things up. It probably wasn't entirely safe to leave me alone given that I didn't know how to defend myself and I was exhausted, but the water felt so good that I didn't want to say anything.

A little while later, Cyrus returned and I pulled my feet out of the water, letting them dry a bit, then shoved them back into my boots. I staggered up to camp to find Cyrus turning meat on the spit over a fire and Bishop sitting under the overhang, leaning against the rock wall. Knox was nowhere to be seen, but given how fast Cyrus had returned, Knox had to have hunted our dinner while Cyrus gathered the wood.

"Come here, beautiful," Bishop said, opening up his arms in invitation.

I huffed at the compliment. Even if I might be beautiful normally — which I wasn't — I certainly wasn't beautiful right now, not bruised and scratched up and exhausted. Still, I sank into his embrace, letting the warmth of being physically connected with him wash through me. The achy need from my heat and the mating bond swelled, but, as I'd hoped, my exhaustion was stronger than my desire, and all I really wanted was to lie against Bishop's chest, wrapped in his arms.

This was perfect. This was the way it was supposed to be. Well, not the complete and utter exhaustion or the constant ache from my body, but the sense of peace and belonging and home that seeped through my cells and into my soul.

The guys talked about how much longer it was going to take to get to the death god's altar and what they might expect, but I didn't join in. There wasn't much I could say because I didn't know anything about this world, and while I probably should have listened and learned everything I could about what I might encounter, I was just too tired and comfortable with Bishop holding me.

Their voices lulled me into a sleepy state where I hung, suspended between being awake and asleep until Bishop set a bowl of food in my hand and told me to eat.

I roused myself enough to eat without Cyrus forcing me with his power then lost the fight and let sleep take me while still in Bishop's arms.

The next morning, Bishop woke me at dawn after dream-Knox had brought me to climax with his lips but before my second orgasm with him inside me. I woke achy and needy and thankfully sore. Every muscle in my body hurt and it was easy to focus on my pain and not the thrumming need for a release or the icy hollowness of my rejected mate bond.

I hadn't expected my plan of being too tired for sex to affect my mornings as well, but a quick release in the bushes before I emptied my bladder took away enough of the pressure for the other sensations battling inside me to overwhelm my desire. And while it was the only practical way to deal with the situation, I couldn't stop my face from burning once I washed my hands and returned to camp.

Without comment, Bishop handed me a small bowl of oatmeal with last night's leftover meat while Cyrus dumped his canteen on our dying fire and packed up.

We walked all day and the next, and long before we reached the evening of the third day of my terrible plan, I was seriously regretting telling Cyrus to push our pace. I'd hoped I'd get used to all the walking, but it'd been a fantasy to hope I could get past the exhaustion and aches without resting for a day or ten. And while Bishop had gotten me good quality hiking boots, my feet just weren't used to it and I now had blisters.

But the pressure from the bond and my heat and the achy icy hollowness kept getting stronger, and I was certain the only reason I hadn't jumped Bishop again was because I was so tired.

I'd promised Cyrus I could push through and I would. The sooner we got to the death god's altar the better and not just because I was on the verge of snapping. Cyrus had said leaving town was dangerous, and while I hadn't seen any grimalkins or more flying snakes, I knew they were out there. I could feel them watching us, waiting to pounce, and like a lion hunting gazelle, I was fully aware that I was the weakest member of the group and the easiest target.

Now the sun sat on the western horizon just starting to turn the sky pink with the beginning of the sunset. If today was like the last couple of days, I still had at least an hour before we stopped, and I wasn't sure if my feet would make it.

Ahead of me, Cyrus crested a rise and paused, staring at the sunset. His eyes narrowed and he unclipped his canteen from his pack.

"Bishop, fill up our canteens," he ordered. "Knox says there's a cave up ahead so we're stopping for the night."

"But we have another hour," I said, despite my complaining feet. An hour more of walking meant I was an hour closer to where I needed to be.

"And this is shelter," Cyrus replied, his attention flickering back to the sunset before shooting Bishop a stern look.

"Give me your canteen." Bishop held out his hand, and I unhooked it and handed it over.

He headed toward the river, while Cyrus led me around a jagged outcropping of rock and down a long, uneven slope with enough levelish rocky protrusions for footholds, so I didn't have to slide all the way down.

Another jagged pillar of rock and a scraggly pine tree that looked half alive partially hid the cave entrance and shaded it from the late-afternoon sun, illuminating only a few feet beyond the cave's wide mouth. Without my wolf form, I didn't have the night vision ability other shifters had, but from the sound of Cyrus's footsteps as he march into the gloom a few feet ahead of me, I could guess the cave was big.

"Sit over there and stay out of the way," Cyrus said, pointing into the darkness where there could be anything I could trip over or bang my head against.

"How about I wait here until there's a fire," I offered instead, making him frown. Then realization flashed across his face and his expression grew even darker.

Yeah, yet another reminder of how weak I really was.

I bit back a sigh and leaned against the mouth of the cave, too tired to be upset about it anymore. Right now, just like everything else, it was what it was and there wasn't anything I could do about it.

Bishop returned with our canteens and a handful of branches to start a fire but not enough to keep it going, and Cyrus left while Knox remained out of sight. I'd caught glimpses of Knox during the last couple of days, and last night I'd partially woken when Bishop moved me out of his arms onto my blanket and saw Knox sitting beside Cyrus near the fire.

I'd known Knox was avoiding me, knew it was for the best, but seeing him there, clearly having joined our camp after he knew I was asleep, had made the icy hollowness of his rejection surge inside me and even my sexy dream of him didn't push the sensation back to what it had been before.

Bishop got a small fire going, which didn't illuminate

much more of the cave, and, like the previous nights, opened his arms to me. I sagged into his embrace, but while I was exhausted, I couldn't let myself relax enough to fall asleep.

The sense of something out there, something watching us, had grown stronger the longer I'd stood in the cave's entrance waiting for Bishop to set up the fire, and it hadn't gone away even with the warmth of his arms around me relaxing my body and soul.

Dinner was dried rations from our packs, adding to the feeling that I wasn't the only one on edge. If Knox wasn't able to hunt down anything for us to eat, it either meant there were other things in the area scaring off the smaller game or he didn't want to be distracted from protecting us.

But Cyrus and Bishop didn't say anything about it, and by the time I'd finished eating, I could barely keep my eyes open and didn't have the energy to ask. And really, would they even tell me? There wasn't anything I could do to help. Hell, given the condition of my feet, I wouldn't even be able to run very fast for very long.

AUDREY

Snarls and yifs of pain and Cyrus cursing jerked me into sudden awareness. My pulse leaped into a quick, frightened beat, and my attention jumped to the darkness beyond the illumination of our small campfire toward the cave's entrance where the sounds were coming from. But I couldn't see anything and had no idea what was actually going on.

"It'll be all right," Bishop said, sliding me out of his lap. "Stay here."

I nodded, still dazed from sleep, as he hurried to the mouth of the cave, claws extending from his fingers. But he didn't rush out to help the others. He stopped at the edge of the firelight, slightly crouched, ready for an attack. He was guarding me. Except from the sounds of Knox's low-pitched snarls and barks and Cyrus's grunts of exertion and pain, they needed his help.

I grabbed a piece of firewood and stood, putting the fire between me and whatever was out there.

"Bishop," I hissed, grabbing his attention. His eyes widened at me holding my makeshift club then he jerked his gaze back to the darkness but didn't move from his position at the entrance. "Go help."

"They're fine," he said, not sounding like he believed himself. "I won't leave you defenseless."

A wolf howled in pain and Bishop's back tensed. Fear swept cold and hard into my gut and everything within me said I had to go, help, save my mate. But I knew I'd only get in the way if I ran out there, which meant it was up to Bishop.

"Go. I'm not defenseless," I insisted, even though I pretty much was, especially if it were grimalkins out there. Back in Stonehaven, my club hadn't even made the grimalkin pause let alone stop it, and I doubted this piece of wood would do much better even though it was a little thicker. Still, the things yipping in the darkness didn't sound like the grimalkins I'd heard before. The cries that clearly weren't from a wolf were too high pitched, which meant it could be something smaller. And that meant my club might actually be useful.

The wolf howled again and Cyrus roared. My pulse tripped and my soul screamed at me. My mates were dying. They needed help. I *had* to help them. I had to do something... and that something was to convince Bishop I was safe enough without him.

"For fuck's sake, go," I snapped. "I'll scream if something gets past you."

His body trembled, his expression torn, which didn't make sense. Sure, he might feel an obligation to protect me even though I was a stranger, but his brothers were out there, and they needed him.

Unless he felt something more than an obligation toward me.

His soul steadied mine like no one else's. That meant we had a connection, something deeper than just friends who'd met a few days ago. Maybe he really did care. And maybe that was just what I wanted to believe.

And none of it mattered if Knox died because the mate bond would kill me or drive me insane.

"Bishop, please." Fear and desperation pounded through me, *thu-thudding* with my racing heart. "Help them!"

Bishop stiffened, his eyes widening for a second, then he leaped into the darkness.

The yips and snarls increased along with the grunts and growls from the guys. Someone, probably Cyrus, roared an inarticulate battle cry and something heavy landed with a wet *thud* near the mouth of the cave.

I tightened my grip on my club, my palms sweaty with fear, my eyes locked in the direction of the entrance. Standing behind the fire made me an obvious target and made it harder for me to see into the darkness, but it was also a small line of defense against anything rushing inside.

The wolf howled again, the sound sharp with pain, and my pulse lurched.

Oh, God.

Knox might hate me for accidentally trapping him in a mating bond and could have handled our situation better — although if he'd been kinder to me it would have been harder to resist the bond's compulsion to have sex — but I didn't want to see him hurt or dead. I didn't want to see any of them hurt or dead. I needed them so I could survive in this realm, at least until I got my bearings.

Except it was more than that. There was something about these men that drew me to them, called to me. I thought it was because the bond and my heat were making me horny and they were handsome, or because Bishop was kind to me, but there was something else, something more—

Something that was just my imagination. I was afraid to be left alone in the wilderness. If the guys couldn't survive out here, I didn't stand a chance. That was all. I already knew my emotions were a mess. I was mistaking my dependence on them for something deeper, something that didn't exist.

It was just the bond messing with my emotions. Just the bond. Once it was broken or sealed I'd feel the way I was supposed to feel toward them: grateful that they'd helped me and hopeful that maybe Bishop and I could be friends.

Cyrus roared again and the yips grew softer and softer

as if whatever had attacked us was running away. Then the guys' footsteps drew closer and I blew out a relieved breath. Except they stopped before stepping into the light, making me tense all over again. Was the fight not over?

"You're *not* fine and no you're not just sleeping it off," Cyrus said, followed by a pause where I didn't hear a response, which meant he had to be talking with Knox who could only speak telepathically in his wolf form. "I *know* you're hurt worse than that. Now get in here and shift so we can tell if you need an elixir or not." Cyrus growled, the sound low and dangerous. "You know exactly how big the cave is and I don't fucking care," he snapped, his tone exasperated. "I *said* get in here and shift!"

A massive wave of Cyrus's power pounded over me, bringing me to my knees, stronger than anything I'd felt from him or the others before.

It crushed around my heart demanding obedience. I *needed* to shift. I had to.

Maybe my wolf hadn't woken because Merrick hadn't been my true alpha.

But the pressure of Cyrus's power kept building, stealing my breath until black spots danced across my vision and nothing else happened.

Through my darkening vision, I saw Bishop help Knox stagger into the cave, his body starting as his massive wolf, blood dark and shiny in his fur, before melting into his human form. He was still bleeding from a collection of claw marks over his thigh and back even though shifting helped a shifter's body heal, which told me just how bad that fight had been.

The pressure from Cyrus's power vanished and, still gasping for breath, I crawled the few feet to my pack and grabbed my first aid kit.

"Here," I called out, holding up the kit, ready to throw it to them, as Knox sagged to the ground near the fire and lay on his stomach.

Cyrus's eyes narrowed. "Do you know first aid?"

"The basics," I replied.

"Okay, good." He gave a tight nod, his response surprising me. I'd expected him to huff at that. I couldn't do anything else. Why would I be able to do basic first aid?

But come on. Clean the wounds, which they already were because the magic that let shifters shift destroyed everything — clothes, jewelry, and grime — check to see if any of the cuts needed stitches, which they probably wouldn't because his shift had already partially healed them, then apply bandages to keep the bleeding to a minimum until he had the strength to shift again. It wasn't brain surgery.

"Bishop, determine if he needs an elixir then guard the entrance," Cyrus continued. "Audrey, patch up the worst cuts. And you—" He turned his glare to Knox. "You're still bleeding so it's bad enough. Don't you dare shift until morning or you'll be useless all day tomorrow."

I'll be useless all night if I don't shift back, Knox growled.

Now it was his turn to surprise me for including me in his telepathic communication with Cyrus.

"Better tonight while we're in one place than tomorrow when we need to move."

I can handle it. She doesn't need to bother.

Ah. He'd included me because he didn't want me touching him. My chest tightened at that, even as my core heated with desire.

Yeah, it stung that he didn't want my help, but if he was feeling half of what I was feeling, it might be difficult to ignore the compulsion from our bond even if he was injured and I was sore and exhausted. That was why he'd been keeping out of sight and joining his brothers at the campfire after I'd fallen asleep.

"No." Another wave of Cyrus's power hit me and I collapsed to the ground beside Knox.

"Would you *please* stop," I gasped.

The power vanished and I drew in as many deep breaths as I could as fast as I could, afraid Cyrus would unleash his power again.

"I'm going out to make sure they haven't double backed, which leaves Bishop to make sure you're protected, and Audrey to patch you up to slow the bleeding." Cyrus glared at Knox his expression clear that if Knox didn't obey, he wouldn't hesitate to use his power again and make him fully submit even if it flattened me. "I don't want your shift in the morning to take any more energy than necessary. There could be more jackals in the area, so suck it up."

With a snarl, Cyrus yanked off his clothes and marched away, his body melting into a massive black wolf, just like Knox, before he disappeared into the darkness.

"Fuck you," Knox snarled at Cyrus's retreating form.

"Well, you're clearly not in dire straits so you don't need an elixir." Bishop turned his warm gaze to me, the firelight flickering in his eyes mesmerizing me and tugging at that something inside me that I only felt because I'd been afraid they were going to die and I was going to be left alone, not because there was actually something between us. "If he takes a serious turn for the worse, call me."

He returned to the mouth of the cave and I moved to Knox's side, my gaze sliding over his body. He, like Bishop, wasn't as broad as Cyrus and his muscles weren't as bulky, but even bleeding, his back and ass were beautiful. He was all sculpted, sleek muscles, just like the Knox in my dreams. Even his hair was similar to my dreams. It was the same color and length as Bishop's except without the braids at his temples to keep it out of his face.

"Can we just get this over with?" he grumbled, turning his head to face the fire.

I wrenched my attention up, heat burning my cheeks from being caught staring at his ass but froze when I got a good look at him.

"Your face—" He looked exactly like my dream-Knox, a darker, more intense version of Bishop. It wasn't just that there were similarities because they were brothers, they were identical. Twins. They had to be.

"There's nothing wrong with my face."

"No. I mean. I didn't realize you and Bishop were twins," I said like an idiot, because of course I hadn't known they were twins. I hadn't seen Knox in his human form before.

I opened my first aid kit stunned that my dream-Knox was lying before me. I hadn't known what Knox had looked like and my subconscious had created an angrier version of Bishop. It was just ironic that what I'd imagined had been so close to reality.

Except it was closer than reality. It was as if I was looking at the man from my dreams down to the nuance of his expression and the intensity in his eyes. How could I have possibly imagined him in such perfect detail?

"Let me guess," he said, rolling his eyes at me. "In your realm twins are evil or something."

"What? No." I pulled out a clean cloth and wiped away the blood that had been seeping from the deepest wound on his thigh.

"Then why the hell are you looking at me like that?" he demanded, a whisper of his enormous power rolling off him and his wolf darkening his eyes, a precursor to violence. "I can tell by your arousal that you're attracted to Bishop, so it's not because you think I'm hideous."

"Well it's... I, ah..."

Come on, think of something normal. Not embarrassing.

Except now all I could think about was how my

dream-Knox possessed me and drove me to an incredible high again and again.

My cheeks burned and I locked my gaze on my cloth. Except his beautiful ass was in my line of sight.

"Well?" More of his power rolled over me, threatening to make me tell him whether I wanted to or not.

"I've been dreaming of you," I blurted before he could force me.

KNOX

"You've been dreaming of me?" Just like I'd been dreaming about her?

That was not what I thought she'd say. I expected something like I was an asshole and it didn't matter that I looked like my brother.

"Yes, I have, I ah..." Her hands trembled as she taped a piece of gauze over the gash in my thigh. The scent of her arousal grew stronger and my cock hardened at the thought that maybe she actually did desire me.

Or maybe it was just the bond and her heat affecting her. But what her arousal really told me was what kind of dreams she'd been having. The same kind of dreams I'd been having of her—

Ah, shit.

We hadn't been dreaming separate dreams but shared ones. Bishop and I sometimes shared dreams, but that was because we had an unusually strong twin bond.

Which meant our mate bond was even stronger than I feared even though we hadn't sealed it. And it explained why the ice I'd swept around the chain in an attempt to reject it had weakened the night before we'd left. *I'd* claimed her that night in our dreams, not my wolf.

Fuck. I couldn't risk weakening my resolve and strengthening the bond even more, even in my dreams. The odds were already slim that the spell Whil had found would break our bond, and the stronger it was, the harder it would be to break.

I couldn't jeopardize our one chance to be safely free of each other. No matter how hard it was to control my wolf in my dreams, I had to stop him. It would be best if I didn't even talk with her— Hell, I shouldn't even see her. That would be the easiest way to stay in control.

I should warn her, tell her if she saw me again in her dreams she should avoid me... except that meant telling her that her erotic dreams were also my erotic dreams— or rather my wolf's erotic dreams, and so far, while she was awake, everything about sex embarrassed her.

Without a doubt, she'd be mortified to learn I knew about these dreams.

My brothers might have thought I was an asshole for wanting to break this mating bond, and I'd certainly been an asshole when we'd first met and I'd tried to make her hate me so she'd refute our bond and hope- fully break it, but I wasn't *that* much of an asshole. I wouldn't humiliate her, wouldn't shatter the burgeoning confidence that I felt when we crashed together in our dreams. That would only push her wolf deeper inside her.

And she *did* have a wolf. If we shared the dreams, then the power I felt within her that rose up and sparked against mine was real. I didn't know how to awaken that wolf, but I knew driving her deeper into herself and embarrassing her — even if she had no reason to be embarrassed — wouldn't help her.

No, she could keep her dreams, they'd just change. She'd be alone in the grove, but because she thought it was a dream, it wouldn't be a big deal.

Yeah, that was the safest and kindest choice. For both of us.

"They're just dreams," she mumbled as she slid the cloth over my hip and across the top of my ass, the rasp of fabric making my cock go from "yeah, I could have sex," to "sex sex sex, now now now."

I growled and fought to stay on my stomach. If I rolled over, I wouldn't be able to control myself.

"Sorry," she said, mistaking my growl for anger at her. "I'm trying not to hurt you."

I opened my mouth to reassure her that I wasn't angry, at least not at her, then snapped it shut. If I told her I wanted her, right now in this filthy cave while I was still bleeding, the bond and her heat would crumble any resistance or common sense she had. She'd been on edge since we'd left Stonehaven and fingering herself in the mornings and that one time with Bishop hadn't been enough to satiate her needs.

She should have agreed to Cyrus two days ago and stopped early so Bishop could fuck her senseless. But from the glimpse I'd gotten of her in our dreams — now that I knew she was really herself — she wouldn't have had the confidence to just have sex with him. And even if she did, that wasn't what she wanted. It was obvious she yearned for a connection, yearned for someone to see her for who she was and accept her, broken bits and everything.

Just like I did.

We belong together, my wolf whispered.

No, she belongs with Bishop. I couldn't be anyone's mate. I was too broken. My chest was already tightening even though I'd seen the cave in the daylight and knew it was big, bigger than the ballroom in the Residence.

No one wanted a mate who couldn't spend more than half an hour indoors, who wouldn't be able to attend his own mate bond ceremony because there'd be too many people.

I'd thought I was furious that she'd trapped me in a mate bond, but I was really furious that I was trapping her. She might have been shy and painfully insecure about her abilities and her worth, but she had grit. She'd demanded Bishop tell her about our realm and how to survive while we walked instead of talking about other things that wouldn't be as useful. I didn't know how much she'd remember given that she was distracted and exhausted, but she was determined and that spoke to her true nature, the one hidden behind years of abuse.

She'd also faced off against a grimalkin when she knew she hadn't stood a chance and kept pushing day after day to get to the death god's altar as fast as possible to break our bond. She'd even tried to stand up against those assholes who'd tried to sacrifice her to a monster.

I'd given her grief about talking with them because it had ended in disaster and that had pissed me off. But the more I thought about it, the more I realized she'd been trying to stand up for herself.

She'd failed miserably, but that hadn't been the point. She'd tried.

I still couldn't believe she'd thought that guy was her mate. He'd made my hackles rise the second I saw him, and then listening to him taunt her, thinking she suffered from an incomplete bond and trying to get her to kill herself, disgusted me. She deserved better.

She deserves us.

Stop being an asshole. We won't be good for her. She deserves Bishop. But she wouldn't trust that Bishop had feelings for her until our mate bond was broken. And even if she somehow did realize the truth before then, it wouldn't be because of me. If I said anything, she'd just think I was trying to pawn her off on him instead of telling her the truth.

Audrey finished patching me up, grabbed the closest blanket to cover me then retreated to the other side of the fire. I sucked in a deep breath, trying to get my cock to calm the fuck down, and was flooded with her fresh, sweet scent.

Fuck. If I thought spending time at a dinner for dignitaries from other territories was bad, this was pure torture.

I tried to focus on those dinners. From the moment we could sit still, Mom had required the three of us to attend, and I suspected if she and our fathers were still alive, she'd still demand I show up in human form.

She'd probably been hoping I'd grow out of my aversion to people and crowded rooms and take my place with Cyrus and Bishop as leaders of our pack, but the sensation of being trapped and crushed, all the air sucked out of the room, never went away. It didn't matter how much time I spent with Bishop steadying my soul, I was irrevocably broken.

If my own twin couldn't fix me, nothing could. The only time I felt right was when I was outside in my wolf form. It was as if my human form was my secondary form and not the other way around.

Cyrus returned and took Bishop's place at the cave's mouth, and Bishop pulled Audrey into his lap and wrapped his blanket around both of them.

How are you feeling? he asked me as Audrey leaned into him, burying her face against his neck and breathing in his scent.

Like I should be a wolf, I replied, pissed that I was pissed because she was taking comfort in his scent and body even though I'd just told myself they belonged together.

If you can last the night, we can get in a full day's walk tomorrow, he replied.

Because the sooner we break this bond, the sooner you can convince her that you want to do more than help her with her heat?

The sooner I'll know if what I feel is real or the compulsion from your bond seeping through our bond. He sighed and brushed a lock of hair away from Audrey's cheek, relaxing her even more.

Had she fallen asleep already? She'd been pushing herself hard for days now and usually had to fight to stay awake during dinner. It wouldn't surprise me if she crashed the moment she felt safe and all the adrenaline had left her body.

If the bond can't be broken, I've asked Whil to see if she can transfer it to me. But if we can't do that either, you won't have to be alone in your relationship, he said, not surprising me at all. *I'll join your mate bond.*

Sounds like you've already figured out if your feelings for her are real. And I had no idea how I felt about that. I was jealous that she wasn't taking comfort in me, but not jealous at the idea that we'd share a mate. It would be best for Audrey and I wouldn't die or go insane. I could carry on as I had before while Audrey got the mate she deserved. It seemed like a win-win for everyone.

I always thought we'd end up sharing a mate, Bishop said as he pressed his lips against the top of her head and inhaled her scent. *I'm not at all upset that it's Audrey. There's something about her...*

There is, I conceded.

Bishop let my admission hang between us, not ribbing or encouraging me, knowing — because he knew me better than anyone — that I needed to come to terms with it.

I closed my eyes. Now Audrey's scent wasn't torture, but a comfort, as if admitting the truth had changed something inside me.

But it didn't change what needed to be done. The best possible outcome was to break the mate bond and set her free, then she wouldn't be able to doubt Bishop's intentions for wanting to mate with her and she wouldn't be stuck with me.

Now all I had to do was keep my wolf from jumping her in our dreams for the next four days and pray the spell Whil had found actually worked.

AUDREY

I woke the next day still wrapped in Bishop's arms, his bright, fresh-cut grass scent enveloping me. Knox was already gone, my blanket folded neatly beside my pack, and Cyrus was dousing the fire.

For once I was just regularly turned on and not frustrated from a night of dream sex, and my aches were more than enough to overwhelm the sensation.

It had to be because Knox hadn't shown up in my dreams. I'd opened my eyes to the grove and waited for him to pounce, but nothing had happened, and my real-life exhaustion had swept in. Too tired to stand and explore my dream world, I'd lain on the soft mossy ground, closed my eyes, and opened them again in the morning to the cave.

I had no idea why my dreams had changed, but I was grateful. Maybe it was because I'd been in physical contact with Bishop all night. Maybe that had been enough to steady my soul and control some of the symptoms of my heat.

"You should spend time with Nova when we get back. Build on your first aid knowledge," Cyrus said as he handed me and Bishop the equivalent of a granola bar. "There wasn't a lot of blood last night, but you didn't hesitate to pull out the first aid kit and you didn't care about getting it on your hands."

"Ah... sure." I didn't know how to respond. I hadn't imagined working in health care. Although I hadn't imagined any occupation. I'd just been dreaming of the day when my wolf would wake and it was safe to leave my pack.

"See," Bishop whispered in my ear. "There are things you can do."

"Not sure how well I'll handle something more serious," I replied.

"Hey." He hooked his thumb under my chin and urged me to look at him. "Don't diminish this. Not everyone would have thought to grab the first aid kit or been able to patch Knox up. Even if your place in the pack isn't with Nova's medical team that's still a skill not everyone has."

"You're right," I murmured, not wanting to argue with him. But just agreeing with him made my insides squirm.

I didn't know why it made me so uncomfortable to agree with him. But pulling out the first aid kit and patching Knox up didn't seem that extraordinary. It certainly wasn't that important, not in the big scheme of things like surviving in the wild and defending myself and others from monsters.

We ate a quick breakfast and left. According to the map, we only had four days left to go, but I feared those four days were going to be excruciating. My body hurt even before I'd started walking and two days later, on the morning of the eighth day, I had to keep reminding myself that I'd asked for this.

I'd asked Cyrus to keep going no matter what. I just hadn't realized he'd take me past the point of pain into a nightmare numbness where I knew I was hurting myself, but my mind had retreated into a narrow focus of putting one foot in front of the other so I could keep going.

Except there wasn't any other choice. I couldn't seal my bond with Knox and make it permanent and I'd only last for so long.

Only two more days, I chanted to myself. *Today and tomorrow. Two more days.*

I tried to focus on the morning sunlight streaming through the branches overhead and the sound of rushing water from the river out of sight but nearby. If I could find the semi trance-like state I'd been ending up in by the end of the day, I'd be able to ignore this morning's pain and push through until at least lunch. Except I'd never been able to reach that state first thing in the morning before and couldn't seem to find it now.

After almost two and a half days straight of rocky landscape, we entered another forest, and the forest's stillness surrounded us. Thankfully, the sense that we were being watched hadn't reappeared since the jackal attack two nights ago and the stillness wasn't the dark ominous stillness from Darkweald but the deep calm that made me feel as if my soul might actually be half wolf.

Ahead of me, Cyrus hiked up yet another a rise then half hopped half skidded down the incline on the other side, disappearing out of sight.

I bit back a groan and trudged after him. Yesterday morning, we'd gone over a rise and I'd lost my balance, nearly falling face first down the other side. After that, the guys wouldn't let me go down even the gentlest slope by myself without one of them standing at the bottom to catch me, and I ended up with their hands on me or their arms around me and my desire flaring hot and needy despite being sore and exhausted.

Bishop and I reached the top of the rise and I stared down at Cyrus and Knox standing in the middle of... was that a road?

I blinked, but the road didn't disappear. It wasn't a mirage from my exhausted mind. Below was an actual road running northwest, possibly following the river like we were, and east. It wasn't paved, but the ground had clearly been cut away and smoothed. Without a doubt, it was a road.

Bishop skidded down the incline then reached out to catch me and I followed, pushing out of his arms the second my feet were firmly on the road before my desire could burn out of control and I ended up groping him like I had the last time he'd caught me.

"Are we sticking to our original route?" Bishop asked. "This isn't on the map so I don't know if it'll lead to the death god's temple."

"Do we know when that map was made?" Cyrus asked, then he turned to Knox, paused as if he were listening to something, and nodded. "Agreed. If it turns fully north up ahead, it'll make traveling easier."

"If it does go north, we might run into trouble," Bishop replied as Knox bounded up the road. "The map is eighty years old, but unless this road is well maintained, it looks a lot newer than that. Either way, if it heads north that might mean the death god has new and active followers."

Cyrus took a long drink from his canteen, his eyes scanning the area although I wasn't sure what he was looking for. I couldn't sense trouble. With the birds chirping, the sunlight streaming through the leaves and branches, and the steady *rush* of the river nearby, the forest felt peaceful.

"Let me see the map," he said, turning to Bishop. But his attention caught on me and he sighed. "While we figured this out, why don't you fill our canteens."

"Sure." I took his and Bishop's canteens, left my pack with them — since there was no point in hauling it to the river and back — and headed up the road after Knox. The rise shrunk to half its height about fifty feet away and that would be easier to climb up than what we'd just skidded down.

The river wasn't that much farther, and I quickly

reached its rocky banks and fast-moving water. Ahead I could hear the rush of a waterfall, it had to be close, but couldn't see it because the river turned slightly, and the trees blocked my view.

Carefully, I picked my way across the boulders and rocks to the water's edge and was about to dip the first canteen into the water when a young voice, from the direction of the waterfall, whooped and something splashed. More young voices and splashes followed then came a feminine voice calling out to slow down and stop running.

First a road, now a... pool party?

Bishop had said no one lived in this part of the realm, but clearly he'd been wrong. What I didn't know was if they were an opportunity for a night in an actual bed — *and* yes I could admit I was exhausted and willing to delay reaching the death god's temple by half a day for a real bed — or if they were dangerous.

Except they didn't sound dangerous. They sounded like a woman with kids playing in the river, but I had no idea how they'd react to me.

From what Bishop had told me, his pack had relationships with other packs and communities near theirs. There were also other territories and countries farther away, but not everyone welcomed strangers.

That, and the guys had just talked about the road indicating that the death god might have new worshipers. I didn't know what a typical death god worship session looked like, but best guess was that it involved death, and unwelcome visitors probably made the best sacrifices.

But I couldn't contain my curiosity and eased toward the sound, pushing through the underbrush and sticking close to trees and tall rocks for cover until a tingle of energy passed over me.

My pulse lurched and I froze. Had I set off a trap? Did they know I was hiding in the forest?

Someone moved up ahead, but no one came looking for me, and after a moment of waiting for yelling or magic freezing me in place or something, I dropped to my stomach and inched along the ground until I could see what was going on.

It was definitely a pool party and the pools looked man-made like the road.

A small stream from the waterfall had been diverted to pour down into a large pool. The water closest to the waterfall was dark and deep, but the ground sloped up along the pool's edges to create a shallow end and large patio area.

Half a dozen kids splashed in the deeper water, while two more raced up stone steps to get to a platform about six feet above the water. Three other teenagers, two girls and a boy, played with ten smaller children in a shallow waders' section close to me. The smaller children were a mix of babies and toddlers, most of whom were completely naked, while close to two dozen women hung out on the patio under umbrellas, sitting on lounge chairs, chatting, and watching the children play.

With the exception that their bathing suits were more like halter tops and shorts and the material didn't look like spandex, the scene looked like something out of a movie or TV show.

My pack had a community pool, but I'd never been stupid enough to risk going, so I'd never experienced a pool party in real life. But this was what I imagined it would look like. Lounging in the sun, chatting with friends while children laughed and called out to each other and had a great time.

No one looked like they worshiped a death god, although I wasn't sure what a death god worshiper looked like. I assumed they'd be dower and angry and not sunbathing and playing in the water with their kids. And none of them radiated any kind of supernatural essence. They were all human.

Still, Cyrus would be pissed if I just walked down there and ask if their town was nearby and if they had an inn or spare room I could use for the night.

I was about to sneak away when movement in the bushes near the far side of the wader pool caught my attention.

My heart dropped into my stomach, and I raked my gaze over the area where I'd thought I'd seen something. The last time I'd caught a hint of movement of something mostly hidden, the grimalkins had attacked the market and, people, including children, had died. I'd foolishly assumed it had been a young wolf practicing his stalking skills and I'd be damned if I'd make the same mistake twice.

It didn't matter that I had no idea who these people were or if they were even good people. If children were in danger, I had to try to protect them.

A gentle wind teased the leaves making up about a third of the canopy above. The sunlight and shadows danced over the underbrush and the rocky ground, making it difficult to tell if the things hidden in the bushes were rocks or monsters.

Please let me be wrong.

But there, at the edge of the brush, blending in with the shadows, was one of the large, bulky grimalkins that had attacked Stonehaven.

AUDREY

Shit, why couldn't it have been one of those jackals? I'd seen their corpses when we'd left the cave and they'd been half the size of the grimalkins. I was sure my club from the other night would have taken one of them down. The only reason Knox had had so much trouble was because there'd been so many of them.

The grimalkin was focused on the wading pool and not the slightly closer lounge area, and my fear turned into a hard, cold rock in my stomach.

None of the women looked like fighters and I couldn't see any weapons. Even if they were fighters and armed, they wouldn't reach the wading pool in time. I was closer, and while I didn't stand a chance against a grimalkin, I might be able to buy time for Cyrus and Bishop to arrive. I could only pray that with their better-than-human hearing, I was still within yelling distance.

The grimalkin tensed, readying to pounce, and I

glanced around, looking for a weapon. Rocks or branches. Swell

I grabbed the rock at my foot that was about the size of a tennis ball along with the closest fallen branch. The branch was almost too thick for me to wrap my fingers around, but it was longer than my last two "clubs" so hopefully that would mean I wouldn't be within claw's reach as often.

Then the large grimalkin leaped out of the bushes and so did I.

Oh, fuck oh fuck oh fuck.

"Cyrus! Bishop!" I screamed as I raced over the rocky ground, splashed into the wading pool, and barreled past the suddenly wailing babies and stunned teenagers.

One of the girls yelled and jerked toward me as if to fight me and defend the kids, but I ran right past her and threw my rock at the grimalkin.

I missed.

By a mile.

The stone landed in the water with a *plop* so far away from the creature it was embarrassing.

The grimalkin didn't even flinch but I didn't stop rushing toward it.

With a snarl, the beast leaped at me and I heaved out of the way, somehow managing to not get clawed or bitten and remembering to swing my stick as well.

My aim was too high, and the creature ducked and rammed its large blocky head into my stomach. But I'd faced that kind of attack before, and I managed to stumble back and avoid falling on my ass.

Ha! One point for me.

I smashed the stick against the grimalkin's nose, breaking the end off my impromptu weapon and making the beast howl in pain.

Two points.

Maybe I could actually do this.

But the grimalkin surged forward, swiping and snapping at me in a relentless attack, and all thoughts of fighting back vanished.

Just survive, I told myself as I scrambled to avoid being clawed. *Just survive until they get here.*

People and children screamed. I didn't know if all the babies and toddlers were out of the wading pool, and I didn't have time to check. All I could do was keep the grimalkin focused on me and stay alive long enough for my guys to show up.

The grimalkin's foul stench wafted over me, making me choke, and it swiped again. I jerked to the side, its claws narrowly missing me, but it leaped in, not giving me a chance to catch my balance, and rammed its head into my chest again.

My ass hit the hard ground, the ankle-deep water not enough to cushion my fall, and pain ricocheted up my spine. Water soaked into my pants, instantly weighing me down.

With a snarl, the grimalkin leaped and I scooted back on my butt. I didn't want to chance rolling away and getting caught face down in the water. It wasn't deep, but it was still deep enough to drown.

But I wasn't fast enough and the grimalkin's claws sliced into my calf, pain burning through my leg and my blood billowing out into the water.

I swung my stick at it one-handed, using my other hand to help me get out of the way and praying for a second where I could get back on my feet. I had crappy agility while standing and even crappier agility while on my ass.

Where the hell were Cyrus and Bishop?

Then my back hit something hard.

The edge of the pool.

Shit.

The grimalkin surged forward, its maw open to bite, saliva dripping from its sharp teeth, and its foul breath making my eyes water.

I jabbed forward with my stick, hoping to hit its eyes or nose, anything soft that would get it to back up so I could get over the pool's two-foot edge.

But my stick plunged into the monster's mouth, hit something then *popped* through. The weight of the grimalkin slammed into me, wrenched my stick from my hand, and crushed me against the pool's edge. Blood rushed out of its mouth onto my chest and neck but it didn't move. I'd killed it.

Somehow, I'd killed it.

Then Cyrus splashed past me and I realized there were two other grimalkins. Knox was already in the shallow water near the patio, keeping both of them away from the humans, snarling and biting, fighting to block off one grimalkin and pin the other. But it was a losing fight and even though the women and children were running from the pool area, Knox and the grimalkins kept getting closer and closer to them.

Bishop hurried to my side and hauled the grimalkin off me as Knox buried his teeth into one of the grimalkins' throats and tore it open.

A second later, Cyrus tackled the other grimalkin before it could rush past Knox. The grimalkin dug its back claws into Cyrus's stomach, but Cyrus held on, and with a roar — and a strength I hadn't thought possible — Cyrus snapped the beast's thick neck.

"Are you hurt?" Bishop asked, his gaze sweeping down my body as if he didn't trust me to tell him the truth and sending a shiver of desire rushing through me.

The muscles in his jaw tightened when he reached the gashes in my calf. With a low growl, he lifted me into his arms, not bothering to ask if I could walk and not caring that I was soaked in water and blood, then clamped a large hand around my calf to slow the bleeding.

"Two days. Two fucking days. That was all you needed to wait and then you could have done whatever the hell you wanted," Cyrus yelled, storming toward me as if he hadn't noticed he was bleeding. God, even when he was bleeding he was gorgeous.

Water soaked his clothes, clinging to his powerful

body, leaving nothing to the imagination, including how well-endowed he was. Not that I needed help imagining his naked body. I'd seen everything and it was burned into my brain.

"I'd ask what's wrong with you," he huffed, "but I already know."

A woman with streaks of gray in her hair and wearing a loose beach dress splashed through the water toward us. Her face was pale and her eyes too wide with shock, but her expression was serious and determined. She was holding herself together to stay in control, and she was coming toward us instead of running away which made me think she was in charge.

"Is anyone hurt?" Bishop asked her.

She eyed Cyrus then looked at me, and I realized the entire front of my shirt was soaked with watery blood and giving everyone a show of my perpetually turned-on nipples. Thank God she couldn't smell my arousal like the guys could. Still, I crossed my arms and prayed someone would offer me a change of clothes while I waited for mine to dry... because the other option was waiting naked and that wasn't going to help the desire constantly raging through me.

"A few scrapes and bruises," the woman replied. "We should get you two to our doctor."

"Just Audrey," Cyrus replied. "A quick shift and I'll be fine. I'm just waiting until the pool clears out. Most humans I know don't appreciate public nudity."

The woman's gaze trailed appreciatively over his body

and something inside me twisted. "I'm sure no one here would mind if you stripped."

"Mom!" a younger woman exclaimed as she hurried toward us. "You're a married woman."

"Doesn't mean I can't look," the older woman said with a sly smile.

"Oh, goddess save me." The younger woman rolled her eyes at her mother. "I'm so sorry. Thank you for saving us. I'm Hallie and this is my mother, Neera. Let's get you some dry clothes and have Ida check you out."

Bishop glanced at Cyrus and raised an eyebrow, and Cyrus gave an ever-so-slight nod.

"Is your village nearby?" Bishop asked.

"Not far. Will you be able to walk?" Neera asked Cyrus, her tone turning seductive. "Or should we wait for you to change forms?"

"Please forgive her," Hallie groaned. "There hasn't been a new handsome man in town since—"

"Since you snatched up the last one," her mother chuckled. "And now two more have shown up and saved your wedding day."

Cyrus grabbed our packs from the bushes where he and Bishop had left them and our canteens where I'd left them, and then Hallie and Neera led us out of the pool area.

"Are all three of you shifters?" Hallie asked as we stepped onto a wide, well-maintained path lined with what looked like patio stones.

The path led up a gentle slope until we were level

with the river again and, from my glimpse through the trees, toward a collection of sturdy stone buildings. Much to my surprise, Knox fell into step beside Cyrus instead of returning to the shadows, but his posture was tense, and I hoped the villagers wouldn't mistake his worry as aggression.

"All four of us," Bishop corrected. "I'm Bishop, this is Audrey, Cyrus, and Knox."

Hallie leaned closer to us and dropped her voice. "Is he not shifting because he doesn't want my mother ogling him? I wouldn't blame him."

"Yeah, he's the best looking of the three of us," Bishop said with a chuckle. "Doesn't want to cause a commotion and all that."

"Better looking...?" Hallie's attention turn to Cyrus who walked ahead of us with her mother, and her gaze dropped to his perfectly outlined butt.

The something inside me twisted tighter and turned sour. No, not something. Jealousy. I was jealous this woman was checking out Cyrus even though he'd made it clear he wasn't interested in me. Not that I wanted him to be interested. I was just horny as hell from the mating bond and my heat.

Besides, if I was too weak to be his mate, a human would be even worse. And I was not going to think about how much it would hurt if he rejected me but accepted this human.

AUDREY

THE PATH TURNED AWAY FROM THE RIVER, AND THE TREES parted revealing a village huddled at the edge of a large meadow complete with grass and flowers, something I hadn't seen since entering Darkweald. There were still areas where the ground was uneven and rocks jutted from the earth, but this wasn't the same rugged landscape we'd been traveling through.

The meadow had been divided into two areas, the first and larger area was a farm with a vegetable garden, a small orchard, a pasture for cows and sheep, and a flock of chickens. The second area looked like a park. The ground was more level and the grass had been cut. A large red canopy had been erected on one side decorated with ribbons and flowers, and in the center, wood had been piled high to make a bonfire, reminding me that Neera had said that Hallie's wedding was today.

Relief eased my sour jealousy but was quickly

replaced with worry about having such a ridiculous response to some woman checking out the guys in the first place.

God, I couldn't wait for the bond to be broken and my heat to be over. Surely it would be over soon since it had been going for a week.

Cyrus wasn't mine. Neither were Bishop or Knox. I had to figure out how to survive on my own because once this was over, there was a good chance that's where I'd be. Alone.

Three men carrying swords and strange looking old-fashioned rifles rushed up the path toward us.

"Everyone is gathering in the square," one of the men said. "Are you the men who saved the women and children?"

"And woman," Hallie added, making the three men look at me, soaked, disheveled, bleeding, and in Bishop's arms. "She killed one of the grimalkins herself, and we should get her to Ida."

"Right," the youngest looking of the three said. "Of course." He blushed and palmed the back of his neck, looking embarrassed, but I wasn't sure why. I had my arms firmly crossed, hiding my nipples, so he couldn't see anything inappropriate.

"Come on," the first man said, grabbing the young guy's arm and pulling him away.

We continued into town, reaching a square that was filled with worried people. Knox's posture grew even more tense and the fur on the back of his neck started to rise. Thankfully, he didn't start growling or baring his teeth and drawing the attention of the villagers who were already afraid of being attacked by beasts.

At the far end of the square, a man stood on the steps of a larger, fancier building telling people to stay calm, that the protection stones were being checked, and yes, they were sending out a hunting party to ensure the wedding was safe.

Neera broke off from us and hurried into the crowd, while Hallie led us to a two-story building that backed onto the meadow. Women and children wrapped in towels gathered around the open front door and an older woman sat on a stool cleaning a nasty scrape on a little boy's elbow.

The crowd took one look at me and Cyrus and parted, letting the woman hurry all of us inside except for Knox — who slipped down the path along the side of the house, heading away from the crowd.

"So, this is the great warrior maiden all the kids are talking about," the woman said, walking us into a hall with long wooden benches on both sides and into the closest of four doors.

The room was a basic version of a patient room in a doctor's office with white walls and cabinets, a small sink, white marble counter, and a hard exam bed.

"Yep," Hallie said as Bishop set me on the bed. "All four of them are shifters and you should have seen it, Ida. Cyrus here—" she gestured to Cyrus "—killed one of the grimalkins by snapping its neck."

Ida's gaze jumped from my bleeding calf to Cyrus who was holding both packs and not bothering to apply pressure to the gashes in his chest — gashes that weren't bleeding as much as before since even without shifting, shifters healed faster than humans.

"If you're all shifters then you don't need me," Ida replied. "I'll just step out and find you some dry clothes while you shift out your injuries." She frowned. "In fact, why haven't you done that already?"

"Humans have a thing with nudity," Cyrus said, "and Audrey—" He glanced at me and I could see him trying to decide if he was going to share my not-so-secret secret. And while I respected that he was taking my feelings into consideration, I was still bleeding.

"I heal like a human," I said, saving him from making the decision.

Ida's eyebrows shot up. "Really? That's unusual. I took a specialized class in shifter medicine at the Royal Medical Academy, and I've never heard of that."

"It's a condition we're hoping to rectify by visiting the death god's temple," Bishop said, sort of lying, but not... except if the spell could break something as powerful as a mating bond, maybe it could break the curse my ancestors had put on our pack preventing us from shifting until the summer solstice after our eighteenth birthday.

"The death god's temple?" Hallie asked.

"Our wise woman found a spell that we think will help," Bishop replied as Ida cut open my pant leg and drew the fabric away from the gashes.

Three of the grimalkin's claws had caught my calf, the cuts slicing from the middle of my shin, down to my ankle. Even the top of my boot — which came to just above my ankle — was nicked.

"Let's get your boot off for a better look," the old woman said.

Bishop unlaced my boot and slipped it off, revealing the makeshift bandages I'd wrapped around my foot to help cushion the blisters on my blisters. Except the wrappings hadn't been doing the best job of protecting my feet since it wasn't even lunch and I'd already bled through them.

"Jeez, is that your other shirt?" Cyrus growled, his voice low, dangerous, making fear flutter through my chest.

Crap. I hadn't thought anyone would be upset since the shirt had already been torn in various places by the flying snakes. But Bishop had bought all my clothes and ripping up the shirt meant I'd wasted their money. I probably looked ungrateful for them helping and feeding and clothing me.

"I'm sorry," I murmured. "I didn't want to use up our medical supplies."

Ida carefully unwrapped my foot, exposing my many broken and bleeding blisters. Bishop hissed, his expression darkening, and Cyrus growled low in his throat as a wave of his power swept over me.

"I needed to do something," I insisted. Surely they could see that.

"You needed to tell me your feet were hurting you," Cyrus snarled then turned to Hallie who'd gone pale at the sight of my abused foot. "We need to stay the night. Do you have a room we could use? We can pay."

"You're not paying for anything," she replied. "But I'll have to ask around. Our inn isn't very big and my family from out of town and my fiancé's family have filled it up."

"Cyrus, we shouldn't slow down." If the inn was full, I was going to end up sleeping on someone's floor, which was somewhat better than the ground out in the open, but not by much. If a bed wasn't available and I was going to have another uncomfortable sleep, I might as well be closer to the death god's altar. "We—"

Cyrus glared at me and his power snapped my mouth shut, reminding me in no uncertain terms that he was the alpha and I was the weakest shifter in existence. And while he hadn't used a lot of power, he was more than capable of flattening me if I pressed the matter.

"We're fine with the floor," he said. "We just need shelter and assured safety for a night."

"Put them in old Mac's house," Ida suggested. "It's empty until the new village hunt master arrives and they'd probably appreciate the privacy."

"That's a great idea," Hallie said. "It's on the other side of town from the bonfire so my wedding celebration won't disturb you. I'll get some of the girls to help clean it up and air out the mattresses. We'll have everything ready for after supper and you're not paying for that, either. You're our honored guests. Attend my wedding and enjoy the food and celebration." A whisper of darkness shifted through her expression. "Without you, there might not have been a wedding."

"All right. Knox and I will join that hunting party to help ensure there aren't any more grimalkins hanging around." Cyrus shot me another glare. "Bishop, keep Audrey from doing anything stupid and that includes walking." He grabbed his pack and turned to Ida. "Is there a spare room I can shift in?"

"The room on the other side of the hall is also a patient room. You can use that," Ida replied, pouring something that smelled like rubbing alcohol onto a piece of gauze and dabbing it over the first gash.

Pain burned through my calf and I sucked in a sharp breath. Definitely rubbing alcohol.

"Do you need a change of clothes?" Hallie asked Cyrus.

"No, but Audrey apparently does since she ripped up her spare shirt." He marched across the hall into the other patient room, closed the door, and my thoughts instantly jumped to him stripping off his clothes.

Unbelievable. He was clearly pissed at me and I still wanted to have sex with him. I was insane. It was the only explanation. If I was going to have sex with anyone, it would be Bishop.

Except if the bond couldn't be broken, it was going to be Knox whether we liked it or not.

Swell.

BISHOP

AUDREY JERKED HER GAZE FROM THE DOOR ACROSS THE hall where Cyrus had gone and groaned. The scent of her desire curled around her, and I fought my own arousal so I wouldn't embarrass her even more in front of Ida and Hallie, even as my wolf strained to take over and satisfy her.

Exhausting herself and walking until her feet bled hadn't been enough to control her heat, and after we rested in the village it was going to be even harder.

A part of me had wanted to argue with Cyrus about staying. We only had a day and a half until we reached the death god's temple, and she'd been suffering from her heat for seven days already. If she stayed in her current painful state, she might be able to hold out until we broke the bond, or her heat broke... which surely would be soon.

Except the rest of me hurt just looking at her feet.

Hell, I had no idea how she'd managed to get as far as she had without asking for help. She needed to rest and she needed an elixir if she was going to carry on. Even if I carried her the rest of the way, she still needed medical attention and rest.

The only question remaining was how she was going to deal with the pressure of her heat. I wanted to respect her wishes, help her hold out until she knew for certain she was no longer mated to Knox, but given that she was craving Cyrus even in her current condition, that wasn't a reasonable expectation.

Besides, if she was going to give in and tend to her natural bodily needs, this was the place to do it. She'd have privacy, a bed by the sound of it, and time for me to do it right.

I was just going to have to approach her carefully and keep hold of my heart. I was certain Knox's bond with Audrey was affecting me, but I was now also certain that even without Knox's influence, I'd want Audrey.

Because of my bond with Knox, I'd been fighting what I felt, fighting what my wolf knew with absolute certainty and had been quietly waiting for me to realize.

Audrey was our mate.

She'd always been our mate and always would be. Fate had decided.

It didn't matter that she was powerless and couldn't shift — although I could feel a power inside her, had felt a ripple of it when she'd told me to help Cyrus and Knox during the jackal attack.

But it didn't matter if she ended up powerless and wolfless her whole life. My wolf and soul needed her, craved her, wouldn't be complete without her.

Except just because my wolf and I understood the truth, didn't mean she did. And even if she did accept the fact that we were fated for each other, it might not happen quickly. She'd been tricked by the promise of a fated mate and would be wary of it no matter what her heart told her.

That and she needed time to adjust to her new realm and new pack, to figure out who she was and what she wanted. She'd never been given an opportunity to become who she was supposed to be, and her bond with Knox, a bond I knew that was fated as well, only complicated the matter.

If only she'd bonded with me first. She wouldn't have had to deal with being rejected, something that had made her self-confidence fragile. And while I knew she was a fighter and determined, one blow too many or too strong could shatter her.

"I'll find you something to wear and get the girls started on Mac's house," Hallie said to Audrey then hurried out of the doctor's office.

The patient room opened and Cyrus stormed out with his and Audrey's packs slung over his shoulder and dressed in his clean clothes — washed and mended from our fight with Tzanagoth's spirits.

Audrey's arousal thickened, and my wolf heaved under my skin.

She needed us. Now. She'd needed us before, too. It had almost been a week and my wolf was still pissed that we hadn't eased her heat's symptoms on the rocky river-bank just outside Darkweald.

And it was furious that we'd only held her for the last seven days. We'd been so close and yet not nearly close enough. It wouldn't be satisfied until our cock and teeth were in her and a mating bond fully formed and sealed.

I swallowed back a growl and somehow managed to not pace as Ida stitched up the gashes in Audrey's calf.

"Now," Ida said, snipping the thread. "Let's get you upstairs and cleaned up so I can wrap these stitches and your feet."

Audrey moved to hop off the table, but I picked her up before her feet could touch the floor. "Cyrus said no walking," I murmured, my wolf making my voice husky.

Her eyelids fluttered and she shivered at my tone.

"Are you going to help me bathe, too?" she breathed, her desire making her bold even as her cheeks flushed with embarrassment.

"There's nothing wrong with your arms," Ida said with a chuckle, "and I'd appreciate it if you saved it for Mac's house. My tub isn't big enough for the both of you."

Audrey's flush swept down her neck and disappeared under the collar of her shirt — a shirt that was still wet, clung to her every curve, and was currently taunting me with her pert nipples since she'd dropped her arms to get off the table.

I followed Ida up the stairs at the back to a small

apartment and set Audrey on the edge of a tub that, as Ida said, wasn't big enough for both of us, let alone just me.

"I should probably do this myself," Audrey said to me as the older woman gathered a handful of towels from a closet. "I don't think I can—" Her cheeks burned brighter and she crossed her arms over her chest, hiding her nipples again. "Especially if I'm naked."

"Right." I forced myself to step away from her and not wrap her in my arms like I wanted. Now wasn't the time. Not in Ida's house with the woman watching and probably not while she was confused by her bond with Knox. "I'll be in the hall if you need me."

With my wolf snarling at me in frustration, I stepped out of the bathroom and closed the door. My heart lurched, a painful twisting in my chest, and I gritted my teeth before my wolf compelled me back inside. With the exception of relieving herself and filling our canteens, she hadn't left my sight since we'd left Stonehaven and every protective instinct I had suddenly surged, riding a wave of furious anger from my wolf that I'd allowed her to leave our sight... even if we were only separated by a door.

I paced down the short hall into Ida's small living room and my wolf wrenched me back to the bathroom door.

Damn it.

I could wait however many minutes it took for Audrey to bathe. It wasn't like she was going to sit in the tub and relax like she deserved. She was just cleaning up.

Below, the building's front door opened followed by soft footsteps. It was someone light, probably a woman, and a few seconds later, Hallie came up the stairs carrying neatly folded clothing dyed in various shades of blue and a pair of soft tan slippers.

Her eyes widened when she saw me, and she froze in the middle of the living room, gripping the clothes to her chest, recognizing the predator in front of her.

Shit. I strained to get my wolf under control even though I knew it wouldn't work until Audrey was in sight again, or better yet, in my arms.

"They're in the bathroom," I growled, moving into the living room as far away from Hallie and the hall to the bathroom as I could get.

Hallie bobbed her head and hurried inside, and I could only pray she wouldn't change her mind about offering us a place to stay for the night.

Jeez. My instincts were going insane. Even standing on the other side of the living room with the bathroom door closed, I could still smell Audrey's fresh sweet scent and the heady aroma of her arousal that was growing by the second.

My wolf didn't care about what she wanted. She needed relief. She needed us.

The bathroom door opened and Audrey hobbled into the hall with one hand on Hallie to keep her balance and the other on her chest as if she were afraid to show off any cleavage.

Which was ridiculous. The dress wasn't cut that low and she looked incredible in it. Yes, she looked exhausted and her complexion was too pale, but she was still the most beautiful woman I'd ever seen.

Hallie's multi-blue clothing turned out to be a summer dress with thin straps. It skimmed the swell of Audrey's breasts, hips, and ass and hung mid-thigh, exposing most of her sculpted legs along with the ugly black stitches along her calf. Her blond hair was wet and hung loose, framing her face and drawing my attention back to her soft brown eyes, flecked with gold and filled with exhaustion and desire.

The pressure in my chest suddenly released, my wolf receding now that she was in sight again, and I swept her into my arms.

We returned to the patient room where Ida wrapped Audrey's calf in linen, then slathered ointment over her feet and wrapped them as well.

"I'd say stay off your feet for at least a few days, but I have a feeling you're going to continue your journey tomorrow," Ida said as Hallie helped Audrey put on the slippers.

"It's best if we get to the temple as soon as possible," Audrey said, dropping her hand from her cleavage revealing the tops of the ugly red scars marring her chest and shifting to the edge of the table as if she were going to jump off again.

"No, walking," I growled, a hint of my power slipping free, both me and my wolf furious at the reminder of the men who'd hurt her.

She was already self-conscious about standing out by having almost no power. Now she stood out even more since very few shifters had scars.

More of my power rolled over her before I managed to yank it back.

Her eyes narrowed and the muscles in her jaw flexed. "You don't need to force me," she said.

"I wasn't. And I'm not so sure about that. You keep trying to jump off that table and walk," I said, offering her my wickedest smile to distract her.

A shiver rolled through her and the scent of her arousal increased.

I slung my pack over my shoulders, then swept her into my arms.

She instantly relaxed against me, and the warmth of our connection swelled around my heart, steadying my soul as I was steadying hers. My wolf huffed in soft satisfaction. Even if she didn't realize it, her body and soul knew we were mates.

AUDREY

I DREW IN A LONG BREATH FILLED WITH BISHOP'S FRESH-cut grass scent and relaxed into the soft power vibrating in my cells that had been awakened by his embrace.

I was tired — so damn tired — and it felt good to just be held, so I fought my rising desire at being in his arms. I didn't want to ruin it by giving in to cravings that were only going to make a complicated situation more complicated, and I really didn't have the mental power to figure anything out... if anything could be figured out in this situation.

Hallie handed me a basket with food and we took it to the meadow we'd passed coming into town. People were back in the field setting up tables, although the mood was still somber and stressed. I guess the hunt team hadn't returned yet to confirm that the village was no longer in danger.

Bishop picked a surprisingly soft spot in the grass

and wildflowers on a gentle slope at the edge of the activity, and sat, placing me between his legs and letting me use his chest as a backrest. The position made me all too aware of his hard cock pressing into the small of my back and my desire flared stronger despite my exhaustion.

"What's in the basket?" he asked as he rummaged through his pack and pulled out his first aid kit.

I raised an eyebrow at him.

"Pretty sure Ida took care of everything," I said, grateful he wasn't going to bring up my heat since I had no doubt I was releasing pheromones like crazy. How could I not? I was in the arms of a gorgeous man who was kind and warm and a perfect gentleman.

He could have easily started something over the last couple of days while he'd been holding me and steadying my soul, and I wouldn't have had the willpower to stop him.

But he hadn't and that was making it even harder to remember that the spell to break my bond with Knox might not work and a relationship between me and Bishop would be impossible.

"Ida didn't take care of everything," he replied, "not if you plan on putting your boots back on and walking tomorrow."

He pulled out a small vial of healing elixir, cracked the wax seal on the stopper, and handed it over before I could argue that taking one of their precious elixirs for sore feet was a waste. Not to mention it would make it that much harder to ignore my heat. Being sore and exhausted was the only thing that had kept it in check.

"You know this is only going to make it harder to control myself," I murmured and I downed the bitter liquid.

I didn't want to feel better until this mess with Knox was over. That had been the plan. And while I was grateful for Cyrus deciding to spend the night in the village where I could sleep in a bed, being rested and healed was going to make the next couple of days very difficult.

"I know," Bishop replied, his tone strange. I couldn't tell if he was sorry for making my life more difficult or something else.

He pushed aside the cloth covering our food in the basket and handed me a sandwich then took one for himself.

The sandwich consisted of dark brown bread, pale meat, and green leaves that looked a little like spinach. I took a bite and watched the villagers work on setting everything up for the wedding.

This was supposed to be a joyous day for Hallie and her fiancé, and I hoped the hunt team returned with good news. She deserved to be happy. She'd found someone she wanted to spend the rest of her life with and that deserved a carefree celebration.

The thought made the sandwich turn to dust in my mouth. Would I get a wedding? I hadn't thought about having a mating ceremony and celebration, hadn't dreamed that anyone would want to mate with me. I'd only been thinking of staying safe and escaping when my wolf woke.

And then Royce had awakened desires I hadn't known I had and crushed them all at the same time.

I tried to eat another mouthful of sandwich but it didn't taste any better than the last bite.

I'd only get a mating ceremony if Whil's spell worked and if anyone decided they could mate with a wolf as weak as me. If it didn't, I doubted Knox would suddenly decide he wanted to celebrate our mating.

Only his brothers and Whil knew we'd bonded and it would probably stay that way. I was the unwanted mate, the embarrassment he wouldn't want to acknowledge. Ever. I'd be trapped worse than before because this time I'd have no chance of escape, not even a small hope.

God. How could I carry on? Knox and I would have sex, the bond would make us do it sooner or later, but our hearts wouldn't be in it.

Except I had a horrible feeling my heart would be in it. My soul wept for him, and clearly, his didn't weep for me, or he wouldn't have been filling our bond with icy disgust and rejection.

"What do I do if this doesn't work?" I stared at the half-eaten sandwich in my hand unable to bring myself to take another tasteless bite, the warmth from Bishop's body and soul no longer strong enough to steady me.

"We go to plan B," Bishop replied without hesitation. He set his own sandwich aside, wrapped his arms around me, and drew me back against his chest, enveloping me in his warmth. "We get back to Stonehaven and see if Whil can transfer Knox's half of your bond to me."

What the—? He'd ask Whil to transfer the bond to him?

I pushed up to stare at him. It didn't sound as if he was joking, and given how kind he'd been, I doubted he'd joke about something like this, but—

"Why would you do that?" I asked. "Why would you take Knox's half of the bond? Then *you'll* be stuck with me."

I knew he loved his brother, but I hadn't thought he loved him so much he was willing to sacrifice his own happiness to save him.

"Audrey." He cupped my cheeks between both palms, his expression determined as if he was trying to will me into believing his words. "I'll never be *stuck* with you. I'd be happy to be mated with you even if we weren't trying to break the bond with Knox."

That didn't make any sense. "You're powerful. You're a pack alpha and I'm—"

"Determined and beautiful and kind?"

"Weak," I corrected him. I didn't want him lying to me to make me feel better, because I knew none of it was true. "I'm weak. I can't shift and any pups I have could be just like me. No one wants a mate like that."

I'd overheard Finn say as much before we'd left Stonehaven, and I couldn't blame him or anyone else who thought that. As much as I didn't want it to be true, it was.

Bishop's eyes darkened, his wolf rising to the surface. "Anyone who can't see past that doesn't deserve you. I don't care if you can't shift. When we're back in Stonehaven, I intend to court you properly. I will earn your heart and be your mate."

My heart lurched, hope and fear swirling in my stomach. He sounded so certain, so determined, as if I was a prize he needed to win.

The hope fluttered stronger along with a lick of desire. He'd offered to help me with my heat with no expectations of anything else and I'd assumed it meant he was warning me off. Was he actually saying I shouldn't feel guilty or pressured if I didn't reciprocate his feelings? Did he actually have feelings for me? Except—

"If the spell doesn't work or if Whil can't give you Knox's half of the bond, I'll be Knox's mate for the rest of my life." I couldn't let Bishop's feelings for me grow, not until I knew I was free from the bond with Knox.

Bishop frowned as if he didn't understand what I was saying then realization flashed across his expression. "You think only two wolves can share a mate bond." He groaned with understanding. "That's why you've been trying to get through your heat without sex. You don't want to complicate your emotions and risk hurting yourself or Knox."

"I don't want Knox pissed at you if all this fails and we're still mates." Which was also a part of protecting my heart. I'd feel awful if I broke their relationship. I didn't know about Knox, but Bishop had already proven he'd do just about anything to protect his brother.

He wrapped his arms around me and pulled me tighter against his chest again. "Even if Whil can't transfer it, I'll join your mate bond," he said. "If you'll have me. Neither of you have to go through this alone. Multi-person bondings aren't common in our pack, but it isn't taboo like I'm guessing it is in yours."

My thoughts stuttered at that, my exhaustion making it hard to think. "So, you're saying I'd have two mates?" Had he really said that?

"Why not?" he replied. "Our mother had two."

I had no idea what to say about that. I'd never even had a boyfriend and now I was looking at the possibility of having two mates. Not that Knox would be interested in me.

Except I couldn't help thinking about what would happen if he finally embraced our bond. What would all that intensity from my dream feel like multiplied by two? And while my mind was certain being mated to both of them at the same time was a bad idea, my body thought it was great.

"So, I'd be mated to both Knox and you? At the same time?"

Bishop hummed low in his throat, probably getting high from all the pheromones I was releasing. "Only if you want." Then he released a soft huff. "Although not until Knox gets his head out of his ass."

My thoughts jump to my dreams where Knox had impaled me on his cock and pinned me against a tree. Except the tree turned into Bishop's hard, muscular chest, his hands teasing and tormenting my breasts, as Knox pounded into me. The impact would grind me against Bishop's cock and his growls of pleasure would sweep hot against my neck.

Need shivered down my spine and my cheeks heated at the idea of being caught between them... and liking it.

Except Knox would never go for that. He'd never want to have sex with me in real life even if we couldn't break the bond, so the fantasy of the three of us together was just that, a fantasy.

However, being with Bishop and having an emotional connection with him like I really wanted wasn't a fantasy. He'd just said so, and he'd always done what he said he'd do and hadn't manipulated, forced, or tricked me.

I had no reason to doubt his desire to have me as his mate or fear he'd reject me.

I yawned, my exhaustion a heavy blanket on the verge of dragging me under, and leaned back, savoring the feel of his body against mine.

Maybe I should stop fighting myself and take him up on his offer.

CYRUS

IT WAS MIDAFTERNOON BY THE TIME THE HUNTING PARTY finished searching the area around the village. Knox hadn't scented more than the original three grimalkins, and one of the village trackers had come to the same conclusion. That tracker had been the young guy who'd blushed the second he'd laid eyes on Audrey and had proven himself to be quite skilled, which pissed my wolf off even more.

Not only had he looked at her with desire, but he was competent and decent looking, too. He might have been a human, but that didn't mean Audrey wouldn't be interested. She saw herself as practically human. She might think a human would be a good match.

Or, if the spell to break her bond with Knox worked, she might think mating with a human was the only match available to her.

I bit back a growl as Knox and I passed through the

magical barrier protecting the village from ill intent that had been fixed while we were hunting and mentally reached out to Bishop to find out where he and Audrey were.

We'd been too far away to communicate telepathically, and it had been driving me crazy not knowing what was going on with her. Was she being stubborn? Was Bishop giving in and letting her be stubborn?

He wasn't a pushover, but he was so in love with her that it wouldn't surprise me if he let her do something stupid in an attempt to nurture her fragile confidence.

Where are you? I asked him, another growl bubbling in my throat making my mental words harsher than I intended.

In the field where they're setting up for the wedding. Is there trouble?

Only with me and my wolf wanting someone we couldn't have and being jealous over a human. We were leaving tomorrow and Bishop wasn't going to let her out of his sight. Knox wouldn't, either, but he'd lurk in the shadows and watch, not hold onto her all night like Bishop would. I had no reason to be jealous of some random human.

I had no reason to be jealous at all.

She wasn't mine.

The image of her ramming her broken stick into the grimalkin's mouth and killing it flashed through me. She'd risked her life to protect children again, and my wolf was losing his shit, both because she'd been in danger and because she'd proven herself to be a fierce protector.

He didn't care that she was already mate bonded with Knox and, if Bishop had his way, be bonded with him before the year was out. It didn't matter to him that being with her could throw the pack's leadership into turmoil and put her in the spotlight to be criticized, something that wouldn't help her confidence. He was determined to have her, too.

We reached the edge of the field and Bishop glared at me.

Pull your power back before you get any closer, he snarled. *She's asleep and I'd like to keep it that way until the wedding gets started.*

Fuck, I snarled somehow managing to keep that thought to myself. I needed to pull myself together. I didn't want her. It was just her heat affecting me and as soon as it was over, my wolf would calm the fuck down.

I wrenched my power back under my control and marched to the grassy rise where Bishop lay. He was half propped up against the slope with Audrey cuddled against his chest, her nose buried in his neck, one hand tangled in his hair and the other pressed against his heart.

She wore a pale blue dress covered in flowers in various shades of blue. The skirt reached midthigh and Bishop had wrapped a hand under her ass to keep the fabric down so she wouldn't accidentally flash anyone walking by.

For any other shifter that would have been ridiculous. But Audrey was so shy, especially of her body, that the action spoke to just how much Bishop cared for her and how aware he was of her needs.

My gaze dipped from the sensual curve of her ass to the bandage wrapped around her calf and the soft slippers on her feet, and a hint of my power slipped through my control before I could stop it.

Audrey murmured, her brow pinching in discomfort, and snuggled closer to Bishop who glared at me.

I know, I huffed at him, pulling it back. *I'm just so pissed she didn't tell us about her feet.*

You're pissed that you didn't think of it before it got so bad, Knox replied, his ears swiveling and his gaze sweeping over the field, searching for danger even though Rafe, the town's magistrate and Neera's husband, had been assured that the stones creating the magical protective barrier around the village had been repositioned.

Unbeknownst to the villagers, the torrential downpour two weeks ago had shifted a few of them, weakening the barrier, which was how the grimalkins had gotten through.

When this is done, we should send Lucius to the capital of the Birialis Kingdom to negotiate. Their closest god is Alexiares, a god of protection, and they've figured out that the rocks near his resting place can create a protective barrier.

You think we can use them instead of building another wall around Stonehaven? Bishop asked.

If Birialis's king is willing to trade, it would mean we

wouldn't have to restrict the town's limits again like our ances-
tors did with Old Town, I replied, because even if we did
build another wall, Stonehaven could continue to grow
and we'd overflow our boundaries again. *If we can't get the*
beast activity in the area to go down again, there will be more
attacks and we can't fit the town's population within Old
Town's walls anymore, not for any extended period of time.

I sat in the grass beside Bishop and pushed aside the
cloth covering the basket between us as Knox sat beside
me, using me as a shield between him and Audrey.

He was still tense from being around the villagers, but
he'd agreed that it wasn't safe for the villagers or for him
to be on his own, not with everyone jumping at shadows
looking for beasts. Someone could overreact and attack
without thinking and then he'd be forced to defend
himself, which would only turn a bad situation worse.

I was actually impressed with how well he'd held it
together. There'd been a lot of people in the square
crowding close to us, and he'd managed to stay at my
side, something he hadn't been able to do even a month
ago... although he hadn't had much choice today. Last
month at our mother's and fathers' five-year memorial,
Bishop had convinced Knox to try to join us, but before
we'd even gotten thirty people in the square, he'd slipped
back into an alley to watch from the shadows.

Has she eaten any of this? I asked. The basket was
packed with sandwiches and fruit and it looked like only
a few things had been removed.

She got through a quarter of a sandwich before she passed

out, Bishop replied. *But I'll make her eat when I wake her for the wedding and then we'll make her eat again at dinner.*

Knox huffed. *Why bother waking her for the wedding?*

Because she'll also get rest tonight and I think she'll like it, Bishop said. *That and the villagers want to thank her. They've been pretty respectful since it's obvious she's asleep, but they keep looking at us and a mom has had to hold her kid back so he wouldn't wake her.* Bishop pressed his lips to the top of her head and inhaled her sweet fresh scent. *She'll be embarrassed, but hearing the villagers thank her will be good for her.*

I pulled out a sandwich and took a large bite. Not as much meat as I usually liked, but it was fresh and not fire-roasted game or travel rations so I wasn't going to complain, especially since after this we'd be back to whatever Knox could catch, what we could forage, and our rations.

I asked Neera if we could stay for a bit once we returned from the death god's temple, Bishop said. *We have to come back this way and if this spell works we won't need to rush home. All of us could use the extra rest.*

If it works, I warned. I didn't want him to get his hopes up. Yes, he and Knox could share a mate bond with Audrey, but she didn't seem interested in that idea. *If it doesn't work, she and Knox will be mates and have to figure things out. She hasn't shown any indication that she'd be open to a multi-person mate bond so that might not be an option for you.*

She hasn't shown any interest in multi-person mate bonds because she didn't know it was possible, Bishop replied.

My wolf jerked to attention at that and heaved within me. Did that mean he'd told her? Was she open to the idea?

I shoved my wolf back, fighting to stay in control. Even if she was open to taking another mate, she'd pick Bishop or someone else. I still couldn't be in the running. I had responsibilities to my pack.

So, like a coward, I changed the topic instead of finding out what she wanted. I filled Bishop in on the other things I'd learned about the village while struggling to keep my attention on the villagers and not on Audrey.

Kelna, the village, sat on the Birialis' border — a border that had been pushed out to settle Kelna sixty-three years ago. A rare moss grew in the caves near the village that absorbed the death god's powers that the villagers refined into a powerful, highly effective, and safe sedative.

I also learned that the death god asleep in the north was Makaria, a goddess of peaceful eternal rest. Her spirits wouldn't attack us like Tzanagoth's since she wasn't an evil or malicious goddess, but they could try to lure us into a slumber we'd never wake from, so it was best to avoid the death god's lands during nighttime.

More people started to gather in the field, dressed in finer clothes than I'd seen before, and Knox shifted beside me. We were a good seventy feet away, but he was still starting to become uncomfortable with the crowd.

Come on, I said as I stood. *The wedding is going to start soon and Bishop needs to wake her.*

I didn't want to leave her side, but I couldn't let Knox be by himself, not if he wasn't going to take his human form, and he needed to get farther away from the crowd.

We headed away from the wedding area but stayed within sight of Bishop and Audrey. He stroked her hair and murmured something to her. If he'd spoken normally, I would have heard him, but he didn't want to shock her, something my wolf appreciated even if he thought he should be the one holding her.

She lifted her head, her gaze rising to his, and her face lit up with a soft, drowsy smile. Everything within me froze — my thoughts, my heart, and my soul — mesmerized by her. It was like time stood still and I was captured in the warm comfort of that smile even though it was directed at my brother.

Fuck.

I heaved my attention away and managed to not look at her until Hallie, escorted by her parents, crossed the field toward the large red canopy where her fiancé, his family, and the priestess waited. Then I couldn't help myself. I wanted to see if Bishop was right, if she enjoyed the wedding... if she'd want a mating ceremony of her own.

She sat comfortably in Bishop's embrace, eating — thank the sisters — her attention on the ceremony. Her soft smile had returned, but it grew softer and sadder as the ceremony went on. She wanted a ceremony and didn't think she'd have one.

A low growl bubbled in my throat. I wanted to kill those assholes who'd raised her, who'd made her think she was worthless because she was powerless. It made me furious that she didn't even think love was possible.

Of course, Knox wasn't helping by rejecting their bond, but Knox was almost as broken as Audrey was and thought being bonded to him would be bad for her.

The ceremony finished and the celebration began. Platters of food were laid out on long tables and the bonfire was lit. Hallie brought her new husband to Audrey and they thanked her for saving their wedding, making Audrey dip her head, her cheeks turning pink with a soft blush.

More and more people approached Audrey and Bishop, bringing them food and drink, talking and making Audrey dip her head and offer shy smiles.

I grabbed a plate of food and rejoined Knox, who'd moved closer to them — although I wasn't sure if was aware he'd moved closer or not — as half a dozen small children rushed to Audrey's side. Two mothers quickly followed with apologetic smiles, but Audrey opened her arms to the smallest of the girls and let her climb into her lap while two of the boys regaled her with a retelling of her heroics at the pool.

More children gathered, and Audrey smiled and laughed and listened with rapt attention. She was radiant, a shy goddess completely unaware of the power she possessed, and my wolf fell even more in love with her.

She was going to be the mother of our pups.

He'd made up his mind no matter how impossible it was.

AUDREY

I sat in the V between Bishop's legs with a little girl who could barely walk sitting between mine and listened to a boy — this one probably nine or ten — telling an adventure story about his uncle.

I wasn't sure how much of the story was true or exaggerated, but I didn't care. His face was bright with excitement and so were the faces of the other children and adults around us, and he was thankfully drawing attention away from me and the summer dress I wore that was cut low enough to reveal the tops of the ugly red scars across my chest.

A little while ago the sun had sunk below the tree line, the sky turning to black velvet dotted with stars and lit by this realm's two moons, and I'd been hopeful that I wouldn't have to keep hiding behind the little girl.

But the villagers had brought out hundreds of lanterns to light the festivities and surrounded me and

Bishop with a dozen of them, lighting us almost as well as the tables with the food and drink as if we were another "station" the villagers needed to stop at.

It had been non-stop since the ceremony ended. Everyone was polite, but I'd never had anyone pay this much attention to me before, and I certainly hadn't had so many people thank me.

It made my insides churn. I didn't know how to respond. That, and even as I sat there hiding behind a child and surrounded by others, I couldn't stop thinking about how I was pressed against Bishop's crotch and how after my nap and taking the elixir, I was no longer exhausted and sore.

The heat building in my core had quickly overwhelmed any ice and emptiness from Knox even before the wedding ceremony was done, and now I strained to concentrate on the people around us and tried, for the umpteenth time that evening, to make myself move so Bishop and I were sitting side by side.

But neither my thoughts nor my body obeyed me.

It felt too good to be this close to him. The warmth in my chest as his soul steadied mine infused into my cells. I was home. I was where I belonged. I was safe.

And I was horny as hell.

My heat was still going strong, stronger than I would have thought possible lasting longer than a week, and I had no idea when it would let up. Maybe I just needed to have sex and get it out of my system.

Bishop accepted another plate of sweets, the movement shifting his body against mine, his hard cock digging against my rear, and my desire spiked, hot and needy, momentarily stealing my breath.

I glanced back at him, but he smiled at the man who'd offered the food and answered his questions about being a shifter as if he wasn't affected by the pheromones pouring from me even though he was as hard as steel.

He'd said he wouldn't let me do something I didn't want to do. If I wanted to wait and see what happened between me and Knox, I had no doubt he'd wait even though he'd said he wanted to be my mate. But if the spell couldn't break our bond then Knox and I would have to have sex.

A chill whispered through my desire. Knox would want to get it over with. It would be a transaction, nothing more, and I had no idea how careful he'd be with me. Sure, in my dreams, I liked being overwhelmed by all his ferocious power, but I knew my body wasn't ready for something like that in real life.

Bishop, on the other hand, had been nothing but kind and gentle with me, and he'd already said he wanted to take his time, so I'd enjoy it.

The mother of the little girl in my lap returned after dancing around the bonfire with her husband for a couple of songs and crouched beside me. "Thank you for being so patient with her."

They'd tried to convince her to not bother me by sitting on my lap, but I didn't mind, and I assured them again that sitting with her was fine. She was adorable with soft brown curls and plump rosy cheeks and had been content to sit with me without fussing since before the sun had set. And then the other kids and a couple of their babysitters — two of the teens I recognized from the wader section of the pool — joined us, and the adults had felt safe to enjoy the party. They checked in on us periodically but the kids were great, and it felt... nice.

There was a small bitter pang at seeing the kids laugh and smile and talk with their siblings and parents, but also a sense of home. This was what a pack was supposed to look like, people coming together to celebrate and care for each other. This was what a family was supposed to feel like.

I hadn't thought about whether I wanted kids or not. I'd have needed a mate for that — or hell, even a one-night stand — and no one wanted to be with a shifter who was so weak. But for this one night, I felt like it might be possible, that I might be able to have those baby giggles and the excited storytelling and the sweet simple questions asked in such a serious way.

"It's bedtime," the woman said, lifting her daughter from my lap and turning to one of the younger boys in the group.

"Yes," one of the teens said while a man who'd been quietly sitting a few feet from us monitoring his children nodded his agreement.

"Say goodnight to Miss Audrey," another woman said.

The kids rushed to my side, a few crashing into me to

hug me, and wished me goodnight before being led away... and leaving me alone with Bishop.

I raised my hands to cover my neckline even though Bishop had already seen my scars. Hell, he might have seen everything just like Cyrus had.

Heat surged through my veins at the thought of Bishop seeing me naked and my breath picked up. Now everywhere Bishop touched me burned with need and more moisture pooled between my thighs.

"I think I should go to bed, too." I met his gaze, his eyes dark, his wolf just under the surface, but he didn't move, just kept watching me, and I realized what I'd said might not have sounded like the invitation I'd intended. "I mean— I— I think you should take me to bed."

Jeez, that wasn't clear, either. He'd been carrying me around all afternoon and what I'd said could just mean I'd accepted that he'd carry me to bed not that I wanted to have sex with him.

"With you," I blurted out, trying to clarify, my cheeks burning. "I want to have sex with you."

Bishop chuckled, a soft, low rumble that made my insides flip with anticipation, then he picked me up, cradling me against his chest.

"Figured it out the second time," he said as he dipped down and brushed his lips against the top of my head. The touch was quick, barely a whisper that disappeared before I fully realized he was kissing my hair and ended far too quickly. "Thank you for trusting me."

"Well... ah..." My cheeks heated with embarrassment

and I squeezed my eyes shut. I had no reason to be embarrassed. He'd offered and I'd asked. It was as simple as that. It wasn't like I was a nervous teenager.

Yeah, just a nervous twenty-two-year-old who'd never been able to ask for what she wanted before.

"I... ah..." God. I had no idea what to say now. I leaned into his embrace and drew in a deep breath of his fresh-cut grass scent, hoping it would help. Except all I could think about was how I was finally going to relieve the pressure of my heat with the most gorgeous man I'd ever seen. Not even the warmth and comfort of his soul steadying mine could ease the nerves skittering down my spine.

"It's okay," he murmured as he carried me away from the meadow and into town. "You don't have to say anything."

He carried me across the town's square and down a narrow street that quickly turned into a dark narrow path that wound through the forest. The path twisted around a large outcropping and climbed a dozen shallow steps that I could barely see in the dim light then opened up to a small glade on a rise overlooking the village.

Moonlight poured into the glade, illuminating a small one-story cabin at the far edge and a path cut through a swath of grass and wildflowers. The cabin had a wide porch that wrapped around three sides of the structure, and small lights had been light in the two front windows and the single attic window as if to welcome us home.

"Cyrus promised he wouldn't show up until we're done, so you don't have to worry about that," Bishop said.

The thought of Cyrus showing up early sent more nervous energy skittering through me. Except I wasn't just afraid of being seen naked and having sex. I wasn't even sure if my reaction had anything to do with that. My body *liked* the idea of Cyrus showing up, wanted him to watch... to participate.

My pulse picked up, and my cheeks and forehead burned. I was only thinking that because Bishop had said he'd joined my mate bond with Knox, that I could have more than one mate, and I'd been attracted to Cyrus from the moment I'd met him. Not to mention, I'd seen him naked and couldn't help wondering what all that powerful muscle would feel like when it was pressed against me.

Jeez. What was I thinking? I was in Bishop's arms and we were about to have sex. Why was I thinking about Cyrus?

Because I was aching and desperate and had put off dealing with my heat for far too long.

Bishop drew in a long breath and groaned. "Keep thinking whatever you're thinking about and I'm not sure I'll be able to make it to the bedroom."

"I—" Now my whole face, neck, and the top of my chest radiated heat. I couldn't tell him I was fantasizing about his brother.

"Oh, beautiful," he murmured, his voice sensual and gentle as he carried me up the three steps to the porch.

"Sexy thoughts are nothing to be ashamed of. I promise. I'm going to make you feel good. So good. Just like you deserve."

He opened the front door and stepped into an open concept kitchen-living room with a large fieldstone fireplace on one side, a bathroom and bedroom on the other, and a narrow staircase leading up to a loft. Everything was wood or stone, the surfaces worn from use, and the furniture mismatched. But it was all clean and a hint of citrus hung in the air. It wasn't too overpowering but enough to tell me the place had been recently cleaned.

It reminded me of the cabin I'd gone to with Mila's family the summer before my dad killed himself. But that thought brought up a swirling mix of emotions that I didn't want to deal with, and I pushed them aside, letting the growing need of my heat consume them.

We headed straight into the bedroom, and Bishop sat me on the bed, sank to his knees before me, and looked up at me. Even in the dim candlelight, I could see his eyes were dark. His wolf was close to the surface and his expression was edged with a hunger that made my skin tingle with anticipation.

I was really going to do this.

My pulse picked up and I dropped my gaze to his chest, unable to keep looking him in the eyes.

Oh God, I was *really* going to do this.

"I know you're nervous, but you have nothing to be nervous about." He cupped the side of my face and teased his thumb over my cheek. "If at any time you want to stop, just say so."

I nodded, not trusting my voice, my mouth suddenly dry with nerves. Then he dipped in and kissed me. The kiss was soft, a tease and a promise, but it sent my pulse roaring into a wild, ferocious beat with a spinning mix of excitement and fear.

Jeez. What was wrong with me? It wasn't as if I hadn't kissed Bishop before. Hell, I'd even begged him to have sex with me.

But there was a huge difference between being swept up by my desire like I had at the riverbank outside of Darkweald and purposely deciding to have sex.

"Relax, Audrey," he murmured against my lips. "Give in to your desire. I'm not going to hurt you or laugh at you or abandon you once we're done. I said I was going to court you when we got back, and I have every intention of becoming your mate." He brought his other hand up, fully capturing my face and urging me to meet his gaze.

I fell into those dark depths, the green flecks bright as if they held impossible sparks of magic.

"Let me take care of you," he purred. "The way you deserve."

AUDREY

Bishop dipped close again and this time his kiss was filled with the hunger I'd seen in his expression. But unlike my dream-Knox where we crashed together and he kissed me with a ferocity that stole my breath, Bishop's passion was warm, encompassing, and empowering. He was holding himself back, determined not to overwhelm me. I could feel it in the tension in his arms, the flex of delicious muscle beneath my palms. This was my night, and if all I wanted to do was kiss, he'd leave it at that.

But I wanted more than just kisses. Nervous as I was, I still wanted it all.

I tangled my fingers in his hair and kissed him back with all my pent-up, aching need. I hungered for a release I'd been putting off for days and Bishop matched my intensity. He raked his tongue against mine and nipped at my bottom lip, fueling the throbbing inferno that had been growing inside me from the moment I'd woken in his arms that afternoon.

Then he shifted one hand to the back of my head to better control our kiss, while his other skimmed down my throat and across my shoulder. His fingers plucked at the strap of my dress and another icy flash of nerves rushed through me. He was going to see everything.

My hand jumped to my neckline in a useless attempt to hide my scars despite the dim candlelight and the fact he'd probably already seen them.

"Hey. None of that." He dipped down and kissed the back of my hand, right over top of my heart. "You don't have to hide from me or anyone else. You're beautiful and these scars are just a testament to your strength."

I huffed at that. "I'm not strong. I can't even shift."

"You're strong in other ways. More important ways." He nudged my hand away and pressed a gentle kiss just above the neckline of my dress where my scars peeked out. "You'd do anything to protect a child and you're willing to walk until your feet bleed to free Knox from your bond." His breath feathered across my skin, sending a shiver rushing through me from the top of my head all the way to my core. My desire turned to a molten heat, not wild like my dreams, but heavy and insistent. "That kind of determination and self-sacrifice is stronger than any alpha's power."

His fingers found the straps of my dress again and teased them off my shoulders. This time I didn't freeze, although I still couldn't silence the niggling doubt that

Bishop would be repulsed by what he saw. It was rare for a shifter to have scars and I had far too many.

But he didn't hesitate as he slowly drew the fabric lower until just my nipples were covered. Then he teased the tops of my breasts until those tight buds were aching and my breasts felt heavy, yearning for more of his touch.

My breath had already picked up and I was soaking wet between my thighs. And all he'd done was kiss me. I squeezed my legs together, desperate to relieve the ache and not wanting to leave a wet spot on my dress, but then he swiped his thumb across my nipple and all thoughts vanished.

Need shot straight to my core and I gasped. My hands flew to his head and tangled in his hair, and I arched my back, urging him to put his mouth there as if this was one of my dreams.

Maybe it was. It sure felt like it. My body hummed with anticipation, every nerve zinging at the slightest touch or kiss or breath.

Bishop didn't resist my silent plea and pushed my dress beneath my breasts. With a low moan, he drew his tongue over my nipple in a long, heavy lick, that shivered up my body, stealing my breath.

Oh, God. I'd only dreamed that being kissed like that would feel so good.

He sucked on the aching bud and rubbed his thumb against the other, building my need until my breath was ragged and I was rocking toward him.

I clutched at his head, never wanting to let go until his hands slipped over my knees and up the insides of my thighs and Bishop said, "I want to feel you come on my tongue."

"Yes." *Oh yes. Oh my God, yes!* Sex was already so much better than I imagined and if Bishop wanted to go down on me I wasn't going to say no.

His lips curled in a sexy, wicked grin, as he grabbed the bottom of my dress and drew it up over my head, leaving me completely naked.

"You're so beautiful," he groaned, his eyes raking down my body, drinking me in, instantly melting the little tremble of nerves that came with being naked in front of him. "And your scent—"

He slid his palms up my thighs again, urging me wider to make room for him, and dipped in to press his nose against my mound and breathe in my scent.

"You smell like home."

His words swept heat around my heart, filling me with that warmth and calm and surety that I always felt when he held me as if our souls recognized each other... as if we were meant for each other.

Then he inched his nose lower and teased his tongue against me and all the warmth and calm roared into hot aching desperate need.

"Fuck, you taste good," he groaned then swiped his tongue over me again.

This time, the tip of his tongue flicked over my clit, and a jolt of liquid heat swept through me. My inner muscles fluttered and Bishop hummed a satisfied rumble that sounded more wolf than man.

He licked and sucked, turning that heat into a raging inferno. I didn't know what to do with my hands, so I clutched the blanket beneath me. My breath heaved, ragged and desperate from the pleasure and my hips started rocking into him, eager for more, eager for that final push that would send me careening over the edge.

And then he slid a finger inside me, found that magic spot, and sucked on my clit.

Every muscle in my body contracted and glorious sensation rushed through me as strong as my dreams. I'd been so wrong. I'd thought the fantasy was just that, a fantasy, and reality would disappoint me, but God— Why had I fought this?

Oh, right. Mated to his brother.

But that was no longer a problem. Even if the bond couldn't be broken, I could still be with Bishop. Monogamy wasn't my only option in this realm and I could only hope Knox would understand.

Gasping, I glanced down at Bishop who was still between my thighs slowly lapping at my sex and sending soft ripples of pleasure through me. His eyes were fully dark and they held a wicked gleam that sent more ripples rushing through me.

"Oh, yes," I breathed, reaching for him in invitation to move up my body and take me like his look implied.

"Not yet." He flicked his tongue over my clit, stealing

my breath with a jolt of sensation. "I want to taste one more."

"One more?"

"Yeah." He raked his tongue over me and my eyes rolled back.

Oh. My. God.

A long moan escaped my lips, and he worked me up again with lips and tongue and fingers. This time, he teased me, bringing me to the edge, backing off, and bringing me to the edge again and again until I was panting and moaning and begging for release.

One more thrust of his fingers, and I was crashing over the edge, lights flashing behind my lids, a strangled cry caught in my throat. I spun around and around, riding a wave of incredible bliss that was stronger than even the ones in my fantasy.

When I finally managed to catch my breath and open my eyes, Bishop was standing and looking down at me.

"That's what I love to see," he purred.

I squirmed under his gaze, more ripples sweeping from my head down my body as if I was still on the edge, still ready for more. And yet I was also boneless and satiated and so incredibly relaxed.

His smile deepened and he pulled off his shirt, revealing his stunning, sculpted chest and abs. But before my gaze could drop any lower, he captured my lips in a searing, breathtaking kiss. Fabric rustled and I was sure he'd stepped out of his pants, but I couldn't focus beyond his lips.

He tasted like he had when I'd kissed him before, but also like something else that could have only been my release.

With a rumble, he grabbed my hips and urged me to move up on the bed. We shifted, never breaking our kiss, and ended up with me on my back and Bishop braced over me.

The kiss reignited the dying embers of my desire, and I clutched at his powerful, muscular shoulders, my hips rocking up, pressing against his hardened length, greedy for more, for all of it.

Bishop growled and his canines extended, grazing my bottom lip as he slid his length against me, grinding against my clit. Sparks flared inside me from the friction, drawing gasping moans that he devoured.

"Do you want this?" he asked, his voice rough, his body trembling with his control. "You can still say no."

"Bishop, please." I ground my hips against him, trying to get him where I needed him. "I said yes and I still say yes."

"Thank the Sisters," he gasped and shifted to press the head of his cock at my entrance.

I froze, my nerves returning, but he captured my lips again. He kissed me breathless, stealing all thought, adding to the fire once again rushing through my body, and slowly pushed inside me.

It was the most incredible feeling, pressure and heat and a building of that achy need that screamed to be released.

When he was buried all the way in, he paused, letting my body adjust to him, and broke off the kiss to look me in the eyes again. "Are you okay?"

"Yeah," I breathed unable to think straight, a tremor fluttering in my core. I was so incredibly full, and in a way I hadn't realized I needed to be filled, and every hypersensitive nerve was on overload, shivering and heating and singing at how amazing I felt.

"Just okay? I'm clearly not doing my job right." Slowly, he drew his hips back, sliding out before pushing back in.

A ripple of pleasure shuddered through me and I released a soft, breathy moan.

"That sounds better than just okay."

"It is. I just—"

He withdrew and pushed back in.

"I can't— I can't think— Oh, Bishop."

My eyes rolled back and I gave myself over to the sensations, to his comforting fresh-cut grass scent wrapped around me, the heat and home in my heart from our contact, and the pleasure building once again in my core.

Bishop slowly picked up his pace, his long, drawn-out strokes coming faster and faster. Waves of his power washed over me with every push, as if by giving in to his passion, he was losing control of his power. And just like in my dream, it caressed me, raised me higher. It didn't demand my submission but built my desire and whispered to that something within me that I prayed was my wolf even if it didn't rise to the surface like it did in my dreams.

Bishop plunged into me again and again, and I spun faster and tighter, until I couldn't breathe, couldn't think. I could only feel. And the feelings were overwhelming, heat and need and glorious bliss.

I reached the summit again, and Bishop swiped rough circles over my clit, tossing me screaming over the edge.

Fireworks exploded behind my lids and sensation engulfed me. Bishop continued rubbing my clit and thrusting into me, drawing out my orgasm until it was almost too much. Then he lost his rhythm, thrust hard, and released a heavy groan. I could feel him pulsing inside me, sending fluttery aftershocks through me, and I sighed, thoroughly satisfied.

I was ruined for other men and I didn't care. My first time was just as incredible as my dreams and I couldn't thank Bishop enough for that.

KNOX

I PACED THE GLADE OUTSIDE THE CABIN, THE GRASS AND weeds catching in my fur as I moved, my wolf heaving inside me and threatening to completely take over. He wanted to go in there, shove Bishop aside, and claim our mate. And I wanted to get the hell away from them.

But the fucking mating bond wouldn't let me leave, the chain binding our hearts together yanking on my soul every time I got too far away, and that made it even harder to ignore my wolf... and what was going on in the cabin.

Every time I got too close, I could hear them — and too close was the middle of the glade. Some idiot had left a window open and with my wolf's sensitive hearing, I caught every moan and gasp.

Fuck. I *needed* to be in there.

It wasn't right that Bishop was relieving the pressure from her heat. It should be me. Me!

I wrenched myself away from the cabin before I climbed the steps and broke down the door. But getting out of earshot didn't alleviate the pressure. Instead, I became more aware of Bishop's feelings, of his need for her, for her pleasure and his, and his growing certainty that she was his mate which only made my wolf heave and snarl more, determined to break free.

Stop, I snapped at him.

You stop, he growled back. *She's ours, our mate.*

And she deserves more than we can give her. Why couldn't he understand that? The bond wasn't real. It had been an accident, and if Audrey had been given a choice, she never would have chosen me.

Yes, she would have, my wolf insisted. *She's ours. She always has been.*

He jerked me back toward the cabin and I dug in my heels. A swell of lust poured through my bond with Bishop, and I was so hard my cock hurt, my wolf not caring that I wasn't in a compatible form to be with Audrey.

Then she cried out, her voice strangled with the force of her pleasure, and I was at the door, in human form, and reaching for the latch before I realized what I was doing.

"Don't," Cyrus commanded from his seat on the porch swing. His power snapped through me, not as strong as it could have been, but still forceful enough to make my wolf wrench toward him.

"She's mine," my wolf snarled.

"And you think you can control yourself enough to not make her terrified of sex?"

My wolf leaped at him and seized the front of his shirt, but Cyrus grabbed my wrists, broke my grasp with his incredible strength, and forced me to my knees with his strength and a burst of power.

"If you want the bond that badly," he said to my wolf, "control yourself. Then you can go to her. She's not an alpha. She's not even a wolf."

"She is," my wolf insisted. If our shared dreams were true, she was a wolf and she was powerful, possibly even an alpha. She just needed to wake up.

"She isn't right now. She's a scared woman whose world has been turned upside down. She has no survival skills, knows nothing about this world, and is being crushed by your human half rejecting her."

"Not for long," my wolf said. "He *will* submit. She's ours. She belongs with us."

Cyrus grabbed my throat, capturing it in one large hand, and yanked me close. His canines extended and his eyes darkened as his wolf rose to the surface. "She belongs with whoever she wants to belong with. And right now, that's Bishop. Have I made myself clear?"

My wolf growled a warning for him to let go and my power rolled over my body, threatening to attack even as I fought to contain it. "You want her, too."

"I want her to enjoy her first time and I want her to stop being so fucking scared all the time." He huffed.

"And I want her to be terrified when she should be fucking terrified, like going up against a grimalkin."

"She's not your mate." My power grew stronger and Cyrus's rose to meet it.

Get your shit under control before you hurt Audrey, Bishop snapped in my head, his mental voice strained. The telepathic communication strengthened our connection and for a second I was inside Bishop, burying himself in her tight warmth.

Get your cock out of her, my wolf howled. *She's mine. Mine.*

Every protective, jealous instinct I had swamped me. I was the only one who could take care of her and I had to keep her safe. I was furious that I let myself take her on this dangerous journey and even more furious that my brothers had agreed to it. They didn't have her best interests in mind. If they did, they wouldn't have put her in danger.

Cyrus shifted his grip, capturing my throat in the crook of his elbow, jumped off the edge of the porch, and hauled me away from the cabin.

I heaved against his hold, fighting to get my feet under me to get better leverage, and my power slammed against his. The force crackled through the air around us. There was no way I'd be able to make him submit. Between the three of us, he was the strongest brother, the true alpha of our pack.

No. He wasn't going to take us away from her. He wouldn't. I had to protect her, claim her. She was mine.

With a snarl, I rammed my fist into his gut with everything I had.

He staggered, his grip loosening, and I wrenched free and lunged at him with my claws extended and my canines bared. There was no point in running past him. He'd just grab me. I had to eliminate the threat before I could get to her.

He sidestepped my attack and seized my arm, but I twisted with his grip, expecting his counter to my lunge, and sunk my claws into his gut.

"Fuck," he snarled and his free hand clamped around my throat.

With a roar, he lifted me up and slammed me onto the ground, his power aiding his strength and crushing inside my chest.

The impact knocked the breath from my lungs and before I could jump up and attack again, he rammed his fist into the side of my head.

The world lurched and darkened, the force of the blow again aided by his power, crashing inside my skull. He'd never augmented a punch with his power before, and it was more powerful than anything I'd ever felt from him.

Holy fuck. I'd known he was stronger than me, but I hadn't thought it was by that much, and I'd never have thought to augment my blow with the power that let me force other shifters to submit to me.

Then I blinked and we were in the woods, the cabin

barely visible through the trees, and my mating bond was stretched painfully thin. He'd knocked me out?

He'd knocked me out and taken me away from her!

Roaring, I leaped at him, my wolf furious, my skin aching on the verge of shifting back into my wolf form.

"Sit," he commanded, crushing me with the full force of his power. I stumbled to a halt before reaching him and strained to resist, strained to show him I was strong enough to be her mate, and strained to get back to her, claim her, and protect her.

No, my wolf did. It wasn't me. I didn't want her—

Well, a small part of my human soul did, and I wasn't sure if that was just Bishop's influence or not. But that didn't matter. I couldn't be the mate she deserved. I had to keep remembering that. I couldn't let my wolf take over and fuck up her life. I had to set her free.

No, my wolf screamed. *I have to protect her. Mine.*

"I. Said. Sit." Cyrus's power surged, wrenching me to the ground. "You *will* let them have this and you *will* get your wolf under control." A hint of fear filled Cyrus's gaze before vanishing behind his hard, in-control alpha mask.

Shit. I hadn't seen Cyrus afraid like that since Bishop had brought me back from being feral.

Was I that close? I hadn't thought I was. But then, I hadn't realized I was losing control the last time.

Fuck. This was why I had to break the mating bond. I was ready to kill my brothers just to be with her. It didn't make sense. Bishop was making her happy which should make me happy. That was how it had worked with our fathers and mother.

But no. My wolf was furious and I didn't know if I'd be able to stay in control for two more days.

"You have to collar him," I forced out, even as my wolf tried to clamp my mouth shut and control me.

Cyrus's eyes widened in surprise. Collaring the wolf half of a shifter's soul was painful. It wasn't the sharp, agonizing pain of being hurt, but the crushing emptiness of being cut off from a primal part of yourself. It took an extremely powerful alpha to do it and wasn't permanent so it couldn't be used as a reliable punishment, but it could help in short term, desperate situations.

He hadn't been able to collar me when I'd turned feral because once my wolf had taken over it had been too late. That, and I doubted he could collar me without my help even with the amount of power he'd just shown. But I couldn't afford to lose it right now. We were in the middle of nowhere at least eight days from home and whether my wolf wanted it or not, we needed our brothers to get Audrey back to Stonehaven in one piece.

"Do it," I snarled.

"You're almost as strong as me," Cyrus replied. "I won't be able to collar you."

"I'll help."

The muscles in Cyrus's jaw flexed and he glared down at me. I'd gone feral once before, and there was a risk that once the collar was released and my wolf was free, it would consume me and I'd go feral again. And there was no guarantee that Bishop would be able to bring me back a second time.

"It has to be done," I insisted. There was no other choice. I wasn't going to be able to control my wolf for much longer. I could already feel him straining against my control. The only thing keeping me strong enough to hold him back was Cyrus's command to sit. "I'm not going to make it to the temple and then Audrey will be fucked."

Cyrus groaned. "Fuck. Fine. Okay."

He dropped to his knees in front of me and captured my head between his hands, forcing me to look him in the eyes. His power rolled over me, a crushing, suffocating weight, threatening to consume me, and my own power rose up to meet it.

I strained to hold onto it, not let it clash against Cyrus's but melt into it, empowering it even more.

No, my wolf screamed, straining to take over my body. *We have to protect her.*

"You have to weave your power into mine," Cyrus said, his voice tight with the strain of drawing on so much power and not releasing it right away. "I can't make you do it."

"I know." It was taking everything I had just to keep my wolf from possessing me.

My wolf howled and heaved and clawed, digging agonizing rents into my soul, fighting to make me submit to his will and claim Audrey.

Cyrus's crushing pressure grew, squeezing my chest and forcing me to suck in shallow gasping breaths. I tried to close my eyes to focus, but Cyrus had already seized control of that part of my body because he needed to see into my eyes to capture my wolf and collar it.

"Give me your power," he snarled. "Submit."

No. I won't let you. You can't have her. She's mine. Mine mine mine.

And she deserves better than us.

I mentally shoved my power into Cyrus's and it, along with his, slammed back into me. It tore into my soul, seized my wolf, and ripped it free from my human half.

Fiery agony sliced through me in a sudden, blinding flash, followed by complete desolation.

I tried to swallow my scream but couldn't. I had no control over my body. I'd given it to Cyrus and he was focused on locking my wolf away.

Then the power vanished, and he sagged back on his heels and released my face. I collapsed forward, a gaping emptiness numbing my limbs and filling my chest. It wasn't the same crushing pressure of our combined power, but it was still damn hard to breathe.

Cyrus stood with a groan. "I'll get you your clothes."

My clothes?

Right. My wolf was collared. I wasn't going to be able to shift until he was released, and I was going to have to figure out how to live in my human form, a form that made my insides twist and my skin crawl with discomfort.

AUDREY

I WOKE WITH MY CHEEK PRESSED AGAINST BISHOP'S CHEST and his arms wrapped around me, holding me close. An ache, not painful but certainly present, radiated from my core, reminding me of what we'd done last night, and a silly smile curled my lips.

I'd had sex.

And with a gorgeous, powerful shifter who'd *wanted* to have sex with me. I was no longer a virgin and it had been more amazing than I'd imagined.

A flutter of desire tightened my stomach. It wasn't nearly as strong as the desire I'd been fighting since I'd woken in this realm, more just a memory of what had happened and how I wanted to do it again.

In fact, the more I concentrated on it, the more it felt softer and sweeter, not wild and aching and desperate.

I released a relieved breath. My heat was finally over. It had to be. Having sex with Bishop had been exactly what I'd needed. I even felt steady enough that the icy hollowness from Knox rejecting our bond wasn't as strong, as if finding my emotional balance with my heat had helped steady all of me.

Bishop hummed, the sound rumbling in his chest beneath my ear, and rubbed gentle circles on my back with his fingers.

"Did I wake you?" I asked, glancing up at him. He looked absolutely delicious with his jaw-length brown hair mussed from sleep and an affectionate warmth in his eyes.

"I was already awake," he said. "I didn't want to move and disturb you. That, and you make the cutest noises when you sleep."

Heat swept across my cheeks and I ducked my head, burying my face against his chest again to hide my blush and breathing in his comforting fresh-cut grass scent.

He chuckled softly and shifted his hand from my back to my head and stroked my hair. "How do you feel?"

His question made my thoughts jump back to last night and I squirmed, sliding my body against his and savoring the feel of our flesh rubbing together.

"Good." *So so good.* "Thank you."

I glanced back up at him and his lips curled into a brilliant, breathtaking smile. "You are so beautiful."

My blush returned with a vengeance. "Stop saying things like that."

"Why? It's true." A hint of playfulness flashed in his eyes. "I think I'll say it every day from now on."

"Bishop—"

"Come here and kiss me, you gorgeous woman," he interrupted, his hands shifting to my hips to help me scoot up the bed to kiss him.

His lips were soft, the kiss tender. It wasn't filled with the passion from last night, but a reverence, a promise of more to come, a lifetime of warmth and love. He'd said he was going to be my mate no matter what and this kiss was a reassurance of that promise.

When he finally pulled back, I was breathless and well on my way to getting turned on. And from the hardness digging into my thigh, so was he.

"We should probably go have breakfast," he said, his voice deliciously gruff with desire. "Cyrus won't wait all morning and I suspect you don't want him walking in on us."

The image of Cyrus opening the door and watching us make love flashed through my mind's eyes. Except he was naked like he'd been after the grimalkin attack on Stonehaven and his eyes held the same hunger my dream-Knox had had.

A shiver of need rushed through me. Boy, my mind was really running away with the multiple mates idea.

But jeez. My heat was over and I was mated to Knox and practically mated to Bishop. I shouldn't be fantasizing about Cyrus. Especially since he'd made it clear he wanted nothing to do with me.

"Yeah," I mumbled, ducking my head and rolling away from Bishop to get off the bed. "That would be bad."

Yes. Bad. Bad bad bad... not sexy as hell.

I climbed out of bed, my feet still protected by the linen bandages and Hallie's soft slippers, placed them on the floor, and gingerly stood up. As I'd hoped, because I'd taken one of the guys' precious healing elixirs, they didn't hurt. And while the gashes in my calf still ached, it was nothing compared to yesterday.

"Your feet okay?" Bishop asked, grabbing his pants and pulling them on.

"I think so. I'll keep them wrapped up until I find my boots, but I shouldn't have any problem reaching the death god's altar."

"Good," he replied as he leveled a hard look at me. "And on our way home, you're going to tell us to stop when they start to bother you, so you don't permanently hurt yourself."

"I promise." If, of course, the bond was broken and we didn't need to hurry back to Whil to see if she could transfer it to Bishop.

Bishop's eyes narrowed.

"Promise," I insisted, grabbing the dress Hallie had given me — since I didn't know where my clothes were or if they'd even been cleaned.

Bishop huffed as I pulled on the dress.

"You're a terrible liar," he said. "But I get it. Neither you nor Knox asked to be bonded together."

And I'd promised myself I would do everything in my power to free him. I still wasn't sure if he blamed me or not. Sure, he'd said he didn't, but he'd been cold and distant and angry with me since the beginning — so very very angry — and the sense I got from him through the bond hadn't changed.

"Come on," Bishop said, pulling me from my thoughts, and we stepped out of the bedroom into the kitchen-living room.

Cyrus sat at the worn wooden kitchen table, eating a muffin with an apple core with a hank of grapes on the plate in front of him.

"They didn't know when we'd be up," he said, pointing to a basket at the center of the table. "So, they brought fruits and breads. Nothing that needed to be kept warm."

"No meat?" Bishop asked.

"They're not shifters. It probably didn't occur to them that we need extra protein." He shrugged and nudged the basket in our direction. "I'm just grateful for a bed and fresh food."

"Not complaining," Bishop said, pulling out the chair beside Cyrus and gesturing for me to sit. "Just commenting."

I sat and grabbed the first muffin I saw from the basket, not caring what kind it was. Cyrus was too close, but I couldn't have refused the seat without drawing more attention to myself. As it was, I felt like I had a neon sign on my forehead flashing "I had sex," and I couldn't stop myself from blushing.

My reaction was ridiculous and embarrassing. I was an adult. I could have sex with whoever I wanted, when-

ever I wanted, and it didn't matter if Cyrus had heard us...
or if I'd fantasized about him joining us this morning.

My blush grew hotter and swept down my throat and
across my chest.

Oh. My. God.

"I talked to Rafe while you two were entertaining the
villagers at the wedding and he says there are the remains
of a village just outside Makaria's circle of influence,"
Cyrus said. "It's three-quarters of a full day's hike, but just
like Anakar, it's half a day to the temple."

"So, we make camp in the remains of this village,
avoid running into any spirits after dark, and get to the
altar tomorrow afternoon," Bishop said before taking a
big bite of an apple.

A day and a half and then Knox and I would be free.
God, I couldn't wait. And then Bishop and I could figure
out our relationship—

Although now that I had a clearer head, maybe I
should figure out myself before anything else. I really had
no idea what I was doing or where my life was going.
Once I was free, who was I? I didn't want to be the same
Audrey who'd been betrayed by my pack, but I had no
idea where I fit in this new one.

Bishop had said he didn't care that I was weak, but
from the conversation I'd overheard in the hospital, not
everyone felt that way. Did I care? If I was Bishop's mate,
it might not matter.

Except others would look down on him for willingly
mating with a shifter who couldn't even shift, and I didn't

want to just be "Bishop's-mate-Audrey." I wanted to be more. I wanted to be "Audrey" without anyone else attached to my identity.

But before I could figure any of that out, I needed to walk up to that death god's altar and murder my mating bond.

AUDREY

Cyrus and Bishop talked about their supplies and the path they were going to take to get to the abandoned village, and I ate my breakfast without saying a word. Just like all the times before, I didn't have anything to offer to the conversation, so I just stayed out of their way.

When I was done, I gathered up their plates, washed, and dried them, then set them on the counter beside the sink while they talked about returning to Kelna for another night in a bed and resupplying.

Someone had returned my clothes, cleaned of the blood and grime from hiking for seven days and from fighting a grimalkin. They sat in a neat pile on the edge of the couch, right in front of my cleaned boots, and I gathered them, hurried into the bedroom, and changed then turned my attention to my injuries.

I wasn't sure if the gashes in my calf were fully healed so I didn't bother unwrapping the bandage to check. The linen was clean without any sign of blood and my pant leg covered it, so I decided not to touch it and to wait until we returned to Kelna just in case. I didn't want to risk an infection and use up another elixir when it could be easily prevented.

For my feet, I carefully unwrapped them and confirmed that my blisters were healed. They hadn't been as deep as the gashes, even if they'd been as painful, and I was relieved I was going to be able to walk, and not limp, the rest of the way to the death god's altar.

I was just finishing rewrapping them and carefully pushing them into my boots when someone knocked on the door.

"You ready to go?" Bishop asked.

"Yep," I replied, hurrying back into the living room. "And before you ask, yes my feet are healed."

"What about your calf?" He headed to the front door where our packs waited for us.

"Still a little sore, but a lot better than yesterday," I said, following him. "I didn't want to risk unwrapping it, finding there was a chance they could open up, and then doing a crappy job of wrapping it back up again."

He huffed, picked up my pack, and handed it to me. "I'm sure you wouldn't have had a problem rewrapping it. You patched Knox up after the jackal fight."

"Taping gauze over wounds that are going to heal in a few hours is different than securing a bandage that needs to withstand walking for a day or more."

"It is," he said picking up his own pack and stepping

outside. "And I'm confident you would have been able to do it. You're more capable than you think you are."

"You're just saying that because—" I stopped dead in my tracks.

Knox stood at the bottom of the stairs in his human form. The resemblance to Bishop was uncanny. They had the same brown eyes flecked with green, beautiful sculpted features, identical builds, and even the same haircut. The only difference was Bishop kept his hair braided back from his face and Knox didn't. Oh, and Knox glowered like he wanted to rip something — probably me — apart.

Except his eyes weren't dark. His wolf wasn't fighting to take control. And that, along with the fact that he was actually fully clothed as if he was planning on staying in his human form, shocked me the most.

"You're human," I gasped, the idiotic, obvious words jumping out of my mouth before I could stop them.

I'd only seen him in his human form once — my dreams not included — and that had been a few days ago. Hell, I'd barely seen him at all since I'd accidentally mate bonded with him. He'd been avoiding me even while we'd been traveling together.

"I'm not a human. I'm a shifter," he snarled as he snatched my pack and walked away with it.

What the—

Why was he carrying my pack? It wasn't as if he'd suddenly changed his mind about me and wanted to be nice. The icy hollowness from our frozen bond was as strong as ever. He didn't want me. And I didn't want him or his help.

"I can carry my own pack," I called after him, but he just huffed and stormed into the forest.

"Come on." Cyrus jerked his chin, indicating that we should follow Knox, and not addressing the fact that he'd just walked off with my pack. "It's already well after dawn and it would be nice to get to this abandoned village before nightfall."

We walked until late afternoon only stopping for a quick lunch of dried meat and fruit before heading out again. Knox stayed in human form for the entire time, but he didn't join us for lunch and was always thirty or more feet ahead of us.

He also didn't return my pack and the only thing I could think of that would explain his behavior was that he didn't want to risk me slowing him down. He wanted to get to the death god's altar by noon tomorrow and be free of me, and I was too weak and pathetic to keep up. Which meant he had to carry my pack and as a result had to stay in human form.

And that was fine by me. Really. At least as far as my mind was concerned. I hadn't asked for the help, so I was still staying out of Cyrus's way and keeping up without complaint. My heart and soul, however, wept at the icy hollowness of his rejection and the thought that soon our connection would be shattered.

But I knew that grief wasn't my real emotion. I'd never wanted to be with someone who didn't want me.

Even if it made my life better or easier, I'd never want that.

Besides, I had someone who *did* want me, and I couldn't wait to be free so I could be with him. That thought made it impossible to stop thinking about last night or to stop stealing glances at Bishop.

Shivers of remembered pleasure and waves of heated embarrassment rushed from my head to my toes every time our eyes met, and it took everything I had to concentrate on hiking over the uneven terrain and not falling on my face.

After lunch, the forest gave way to a barren, rocky wasteland that stretched as far as I could see. Only a few scraggly shrubs and weeds managed to grow, and I wasn't sure if *growing* was the right word since they were brown and brittle like it was winter and not the beginning of summer.

By late afternoon, we reached the long-abandoned village which turned out to be the barely standing remains of a dozen structures. All of them had been small, one-story buildings, and had long-ago lost their roofs. More than half had walls left standing, but those walls only reached waist or shoulder high and the rest had fallen over.

Cyrus picked the sturdiest looking house, a one-room building that hadn't been more than a thirty-by-thirty-foot box. One of the walls had been taken out by a neighboring house — if the rubble taking up half the floor space was any indication. But unlike the other house that didn't have as much debris, this one's two walls offered shelter from the wind. And while the wind wasn't strong at the moment — just enough to make me wish I had a light jacket — that could easily change once the sun had set.

"Bishop," Cyrus said, dropping his pack and pulling off his shirt. "You and Audrey gather firewood. Knox, see if you can find a well with safe water. I'll get us dinner."

He dropped his pants, giving me a front row show to his powerful, stunning body, and a rush of remembered pleasure shuddered through me, momentarily stealing my breath.

I turned away from him as he shifted, my cheeks heating, and listened as he ran away from our shelter on four legs. Beside me, Knox snorted, dropped my pack, grabbed the canteens, and left as well.

"I still can't believe you blush every time someone gets naked," Bishop chuckled.

"Yeah, well, you like it when I blush when *you* get naked." It wasn't much of a comeback, but it was the best I could think of while my brain was still short-circuiting on Cyrus's naked body and what it would feel like to have all that powerful muscle wrapped around me.

"That I do." He flashed me a heart-stopping smile.

I jerked away, my face suddenly on fire, caught my toe in the rubble, and careened forward.

But Bishop seized my wrist and yanked me tight against him, his arm wrapped protectively around me before I hit the ground.

Need shivered down my spine and my pulse stalled as his scent flooded my nostrils. One night with Bishop hadn't been nearly enough, and I couldn't wait to get back to Kelna and some privacy to go again. This time without the pressure of my heat egging me on.

"So, no flirting while you're trying to walk," he laughed. "I'll have to remember that."

"I can walk just fine. Even if you flirt with me." I rolled my eyes at myself. I'd just tripped because he'd smiled at me. "Okay, so maybe I'm a little distracted."

"Just a little?"

I huffed. "Fine. A lot distracted." I hadn't been able to stop thinking about last night and I wasn't sure I wanted to. Something good and amazing had finally happened to me and I never wanted to forget it.

"Is it your heat?" he asked as he tightened his embrace and pressed his lips against the top of my head.

I melted against him, letting the warm calm of being held seep into my soul.

Sure, I was a little turned on and yearned for another hot night in bed, but the feeling wasn't nearly as strong as it had been before, it felt more like a desire to be with Bishop again, not jump the first hot guy I came across.

Which had to mean my heat had broken. Finally. It had gone on for at least seven days and was finally done.

"I don't think it's my heat. I don't feel desperate or needy at all anymore. I just—" Another shiver of pleasure teased through me. "I keep remembering last night."

"So, you enjoyed it?"

"Do you really have to ask? I'm pretty sure I've spent all day with a stupid grin on my face while making moon eyes at you."

He laughed, the sound rich and welcoming. "Yeah, you have been. I just wanted to check." Then he released me and stepped back, his hand finding mine and gently squeezing. "Hopefully that was all you needed to tip you over the edge and break your heat."

"Yeah." Icy fear flickered through me. Was this where he told me it didn't mean anything? That he was just helping me out because my heat was driving me crazy?

I tried to push that thought aside. He'd said he was going to court me. He'd promised.

But Royce had made promises as well, and all my life, no one had wanted me.

"Don't you dare go there," Bishop said, hooking his finger under my chin and forcing me to meet his gaze.

"I know it's stupid and it isn't true." But I just couldn't help it. I might have felt steadier since having sex, but the icy hollowness and the soul-deep grief of having my mate bond rejected were still there. I was still afraid that Bishop was going to rip the rug right out from under me, just like Royce had.

"It isn't stupid," he said, his voice soft and his expression sad. "You were betrayed in the worst way and nothing has been easy for you. It's going to take time for you to believe that I'm not going anywhere and that you deserve so much more than what you'd been given."

"Yeah," I repeated, uncertain what to say to that.

"I'll wait for however long it takes, and I *will* show you every day that you are more than what everyone says you are and that you deserve to be happy."

Tears burned my eyes and my throat tightened. I wanted so desperately to believe him, wanted to believe that I could be worthy of being loved, but I couldn't make the tiny voice in the back of my head shut the fuck up.

"I'll wait for you, Audrey." He brushed his lips against my forehead and wrapped me in his embrace again. "I'll always wait for you."

AUDREY

I clung to Bishop, silent tears trickling down my cheeks and soaking into his shirt. Hope was such a dangerous, fragile thing, and I couldn't withstand the terror of having it shattered again.

Bishop murmured soothing nonsense to me as he stroked my hair, and his soul warmed and steadied mine. I wasn't sure how long we stood like that before I eased out of his embrace, but thankfully it was before Knox and Cyrus returned.

I didn't want to deal with anything they might say or even the looks they'd give me. They thought I was weak, and crying over being told I wasn't alone and that someone cared for me, was probably pathetic in their eyes.

"Let's see if we can find enough wood for a fire," I said, wiping my face on my sleeve.

"Yeah." Bishop swept his gaze at the desolation

around us and sighed. "Although I don't have a lot of hope for that. I think the best we hope for is enough to cook whatever Cyrus catches... if there's anything out there to catch."

We picked our way through the rubble, searching for anything that was more than a handful of stringy grass, and attacked every scraggly bush we came across. I was pretty sure the branches were too thin to be anything more than kindling, but unless we came across a wooden beam or piece of furniture or something it was all we had — and I suspected, given the condition of the buildings, that anything wooden had rotted away a long time ago.

"Ah, here's a big one," Bishop exclaimed as he peeked through the window of one of the best-preserved walls in the village.

I followed as he made his way around, revealing that half the house was more or less untouched, standing a good two feet taller than Bishop, while the other half had completely crumbled.

The "big one" was a shrub almost as tall as me with a trunk thick enough to make thin logs, and we got to work ripping the branches off until the remaining branches were too thick for me to break apart. Then Bishop took over, and I went to work breaking the thinner branches into campfire appropriate lengths.

As I worked, I let my attention drift to the wasteland beyond the crumbling walls. The sun was close to setting, the few clouds in the sky turning pink with a warm sunset that I couldn't feel, and far off in the distance, I could see a thick fog rolling over the rugged terrain getting closer.

A shiver slipped down my spine, this one from fear and not from my sexy memories, and I hugged myself against the chill.

"I heard that the fog shows up every night over the death god's domain," Bishop said. "But it doesn't reach the village, and it disperses in the morning,"

Which was when we'd march straight to the altar, cast the spell Whil found, and pray that it worked.

Tomorrow.

I sucked in a steadying breath. Whil had said the spell could kill anything magical within us and that included our bond. Would it also kill my curse?

I sat up straighter. Bishop had lied and told Ida and Hallie we were going to cast the spell to break the curse that prevented my wolf from waking. But what if that didn't have to be a lie? What if I could be completely free of everything?

I could be strong. People wouldn't look at me with disgust or pity. I could be the person I was supposed to be.

"Bishop," I said, my gaze locked on the undulating fog and the hope that lay within it. "Do you think the spell that can break my bond with Knox will be able to break my curse?"

He released a heavy sigh and my hope trembled inside me. That didn't sound good.

"I was hoping you'd forget I said that. I felt like we

needed an explanation as to why we're heading to the death god's temple and breaking your curse was easier to explain than breaking a mating bond," he said, ripping off the last two branches to get to the trunk.

"That means the answer is no." What little hope I had twisted into heavy resignation.

Of course the spell wouldn't break my curse. My wolf was never going to wake and that was just the way it was.

"I'm sorry," he said crouching beside me and pulling me into a hug. "I asked Whil the same question and she said the curse that prevents you from shifting is woven into your essence. Given how the death spell works, she has no doubt casting it to break your curse would kill you."

"Swell."

"Hey, don't give up hope," he said. "After your bond with Knox is broken, we can move on to breaking that curse."

I nodded my agreement, my throat tight, and we finished tearing down the bush and headed back to our shelter.

Knox and Cyrus returned a few minutes later. Both had been successful which meant we wouldn't need to ration our water for the next two days and we didn't have to eat trail mix for supper.

After tossing us the canteens and saying the water was safe, Knox turned around and left. With a sigh, Bishop started the fire, and Cyrus set up the spit to cook the... raccoon? Gutted and skinned, I wasn't entirely sure what animal it had been and wasn't going to look at it too closely. It was food, and I was grateful.

I sat out of their way while they worked, wanting to help but afraid they'd refuse if I offered. It had been days since Bishop had tried to teach me wilderness survival stuff, but I had thought he'd stopped because I'd been exhausted, not because I was a bad student. Now I wasn't so sure, since this was a perfect opportunity for a lesson and it was obvious I was now fine.

I smiled and bit back a breathy sigh before they noticed. I was better than fine and by tomorrow afternoon, once the bond was broken, I'd be great.

I was still disappointed that the spell also couldn't break my curse, but I was trying hard not to focus on that. Knox and I would be free and I'd finally be able to feel exactly what I was feeling, not the heartbreaking, icy hollowness of his rejection.

"What are you smiling about?" Bishop asked as he lit the fire and sat beside me.

"That after tomorrow, my life will finally be my own." Unless Bishop and Cyrus turned on me the second Knox was safe.

I shoved that thought aside. It wasn't from me. It was my insecurities magnified by the rejected bond.

With a grin, Bishop drew me into his lap and wrapped his arms around me, sending warmth and calm radiating around my heart. Cyrus cocked an eyebrow as if he wanted to say something but huffed instead and stared at our dinner cooking over the fire.

"Any thoughts on what you want your life to look like?" Bishop asked.

"I don't know," I confessed leaning into him. "I haven't really thought about it. I hadn't been able to think about it in my old pack." I was the alpha's slave, and if Merrick hadn't been planning to use me as currency to buy a seat at the North American Shifter Alliance's table, I probably would have stayed his slave — even if my wolf did manage to wake. "And I haven't been able to think about it here because of everything going on."

But now my heat had been broken and the mess with the accidental mating bond would soon be over. Maybe it was time to think about the future. Except—

"The only thing I can do is clean," I sighed.

"Is that what you want to do?" Cyrus asked.

"I don't enjoy it. But everyone in a pack needs to be useful." Even my father had told me that. It hadn't just been Merrick and Sterling and the pack betas saying that to control me, and I believed it. I wanted to contribute. I wanted to matter. Even if it was just a little bit.

"I'm sure we can find something you like," Bishop said.

"My options are limited," I told him. "I'm not an artist, so I can't add to the pack's enjoyment and culture, and I can't read or write your language. Technically I can't even speak it."

"Whatever you decide on, it doesn't have to happen the moment you get back," Bishop replied.

I shivered, the night getting chilly now that the sun

had set, and Bishop rubbed his large warm palms up my arms to warm me.

"If you want to be literate," he added, "you can learn without pressure. Our pack has always tried to encourage our members to follow their strengths."

That sounded so beautiful and yet— "I have no idea if I have any strengths. I'm not even sure where to start."

Cyrus growled and a flicker of his power washed over me before vanishing a second later.

Swell. I didn't know what I'd said to piss him off, but a release of power like that meant a strong emotional reaction. He was probably tired of holding my hand — not that he'd actually done a lot of handholding — and wanted me to stop sucking up all his time. I'd bonded with Knox and by the time we got back, he'll have lost two thirds of a month trying to fix it. He probably had a ton of work waiting for him when he got home. Bishop, too.

"House cleaning is probably a good place to start, though," I said, trying to sound positive and not worried. "I'll be able to pay for room and board while I figure myself out."

"You're not paying for room and board," Bishop said. "You're staying at the Residence."

"If she doesn't want to stay at the Residence, she doesn't have to," Cyrus growled.

Except I couldn't tell if he meant that to respect my desire for independence or if he was really hoping I'd leave his house and get out of his way.

"Of course, she doesn't," Bishop replied. "But I don't want her to feel like she isn't welcome once her bond with Knox is broken."

"And I don't want her to feel obligated because we're the pack alphas," he shot back and his hard gaze captured mine. "If I told you to stay in the Residence, would you say no?"

I narrowed my eyes. I wanted to say that I would say no, that I'd refuse him if he made it an order, but I probably wouldn't. It was safer to just go along with it until I could get away.

And I'd learned my lesson. I wouldn't hesitate the next time because I was afraid. I'd run at the first chance I got and never look back. I really liked Bishop, but I still didn't know him very well and I couldn't count on him protecting me from his brother.

"Thought so," Cyrus huffed and he turned back to our dinner.

In one breath he offered me independence and in the next, he reminded me of just how weak I was.

AUDREY

I WOKE AT DAWN THE NEXT DAY COVERED IN A BLANKET AND wrapped in Bishop's arms. The sense of warmth and calm of being in his embrace filled me with a heavy, relaxing warmth, although my muscles did ache a bit from having walked most of the day yesterday — guess I wasn't quite as healed as I'd thought I was.

Across from me lay Cyrus and Knox, both covered in their blankets and asleep. It shocked me that Knox still hadn't shifted back to his wolf, the form Bishop had told me he preferred. It, however, didn't shock me, that he'd waited until I'd passed out before joining us at the campfire.

His lids cracked open and his gaze jumped to mine as if drawn to me, unable to look anywhere else first. For a second the icy hollowness wasn't as overwhelming and hope that he didn't despise me for accidentally trapping him flickered inside me.

Even if we weren't permanently bound together, I didn't want him to hate me. If Bishop and I were going to be in a relationship, everything would be easier and less awkward — or as less awkward as things could get given the circumstances — if Knox didn't hate me.

Then his eyes narrowed, bursting my hope, and with a grunt, he got up. He shoved the blanket into my pack and marched around to the other side of the wall, taking my pack and that hope with him.

Only half a day to go, I told myself. *Half a day and it will be over.*

Knox might never forgive me, but by noon today he'd at least be free, and I wouldn't be able to sense that hate.

We ate a quick breakfast of dried rations, tidied up our campsite — since we were going to be returning to it tonight — and headed out.

The sunrise had burned away most of last night's mist, but there were still a few curls of it undulating in crevasses and shaded areas where the light had yet to reach, and a chill still hung in the air. As we walked, the land grew more even and more barren without a shrub or weed in sight, leveling out to look more like a cracked, water-starved desert than the rocky mountainous lands we'd been hiking, and it still hadn't warmed up.

It was hard to believe that all my hope lay in the middle of complete emptiness, and by midmorning, a part of me started to fear that the desolation around us was all there was. There wasn't an altar to a death god and there was no hope that the bond would ever be broken.

But Knox, who walked a good hundred feet ahead of us, kept going north. I didn't know if it was because he sensed something or if he just couldn't stop, couldn't give up on the hope that he'd be free.

I focused on the possibility that he sensed something. I'd come this far, walked until my feet bled. It couldn't all be for nothing. There was an altar and the spell would work. I would get my life back.

No, I'd get a better life. I was still a weak shifter who couldn't shift, but that didn't mean I was helpless. Humans did just fine without any shifting or magic, and I could find a place for myself in this realm. If it wasn't in Cyrus's pack, then a human community.

It wouldn't be easy, especially since I was illiterate, but for once in my life, I could make my own decisions, choose my own path.

And in a few hours, once we found this altar, I could get started.

Another hour later and I realized the ground ahead of us wasn't so flat. It was hard to see, just a bump on the horizon, but it kept getting bigger and bigger the closer we got to it.

That was the temple. I just knew it.

My pulse leaped in anticipation and I picked up my pace. Bishop and Cyrus didn't say anything, but they easily matched me, and we hurried toward the—

Lump.

It was a giant, three-story mound of earth in the middle of nowhere. It didn't look anything like Tzanagoth's detailed, multi-spired temple in Anakar, and I wasn't even sure it was anything. There were no windows and no doors — at least from this side. For all I knew, it wasn't even hollow.

Perhaps we had to climb to the top... except I couldn't see any stairs or hand and footholds, and the surface was smooth enough that climbing would be difficult. Or at least difficult for me. The guys could probably climb that thing no problem.

"Is this the temple?" Bishop asked, staring at it, his brow furrowed.

Cyrus glanced at the sun. It sat high in the sky indicating it was close to noon. The villagers had said if we left at sunrise and headed straight north, we'd reach the temple by noon.

Maybe we hadn't walked north. It was highly unlikely with Knox leading the way, but maybe.

There's an entrance on the far side, Knox said in my head, and presumably in Bishop's and Cyrus's as well since we all hurried around it to find Knox standing a good ten feet back from a dark, narrow entranceway. His posture was stiff and he glared at the entrance as if he were furious with it.

"I'll check it out," Bishop said and he headed inside.

The passage was barely wider than his shoulders and only a foot taller than him, and within a dozen feet, he disappeared into darkness.

With a growl, Knox paced a good fifty feet away from the mound then stomped back. Then his head jerked toward Cyrus and his growl deepened.

"I'll be fine," Knox snarled, a hint of darkness in his eyes. "This needs to be done."

"Then get ahold of yourself," Cyrus snarled back, his power crashing over me and dropping me to my knees before I realized what was going on.

I fought to breathe against the crushing force, my body bending forward and pressing my forehead to the ground in complete submission.

Knox groaned, dropped to one knee, and bowed his head.

"Better," Cyrus said and the pressure released me.

Fuck. I sucked in ragged breaths, my forehead still pressed to the ground, and trembled at the reminder of just how powerful Cyrus was. Sterling had been able to bring me to my knees as quickly, but never with as much force.

God, was that his full strength completely unleashed? I'd known he was strong, but that was so much more than I could have possibly imagined.

The tunnel is about a hundred feet and it opens into one enormous chamber, Bishop said, thankfully distracting me from just how terrifying Cyrus really was. *A bit of the ceiling has fallen in so light isn't a problem.*

Good, Knox replied. He squared his shoulders, his expression pinched as if the idea of walking inside made him angry, but he marched ahead anyway, a man on a mission.

And I suppose he was. He wanted the bond broken even more than I did.

"Come on," Cyrus said, holding out his hand in an offer to help me up.

I narrowed my eyes at it, wanting to snap at him for crushing me while trying to control Knox for whatever reason. But snapping wouldn't change anything. Flattening me was collateral damage and I wasn't important enough to be considered. Better to not pick a fight with a man who could crush me with a look and put me back into a lifetime of servitude. Even if he had agreed with Bishop about finding me a place in his pack where I was happy, he was still an alpha. He could easily change his mind.

I followed Knox down the passage with one hand dragging on the wall and the other held in front of me, slowing to a crawl once I was in complete darkness. The air was even cooler inside than outside the mound and damp even though the surrounding land looked like it was starving for water.

Cyrus drew up close behind me, a whisper of his body heat radiating against my back, but thankfully didn't complain about my pace. He just remained a hulking, intimidating presence at my back. One that, even though he'd just terrified me with his show of power, still sent a teasing shiver of need rushing through me.

I quickly tamped down on that. It was just more

residual good feelings from having sex with Bishop. Cyrus was gorgeous in that sexy bad boy kind of way and now I knew how amazing sex could be. That was all.

After what felt like forever but was probably only about ten minutes, I could make out the end of the passage and a hint of light beyond. The light didn't get much brighter when I reached the end, but it was enough to tell I'd reached an empty cavernous room.

The edges of the room were draped in darkness and I couldn't tell if there were any other passages, while most of the floor was smooth flat ground. The exception was where the rubble had fallen from the ceiling and the coffin-sized slab of stone in the center.

The death god's altar.

Bishop and Knox stood by the altar, and Bishop had already pulled out the piece of paper with the instructions along with the vial of shimmering golden liquid Whil had given him to power the spell — since shifters couldn't summon magical power like a fae sorcerer or even a human witch.

"Let's get this over with," Cyrus said, nudging me forward and making me realize I still stood at the mouth of the passage.

"Right." My pulse picked up with hope and anticipation, and I hurried across the perfectly smooth floor, my footsteps echoing around me.

This was it. This would break our bond and I'd be free. For the first time in my life, I'd be free.

"You need to stand across from each other," Bishop

directed, and Knox moved to the other side of the altar as I stepped up beside Bishop.

The altar was the only thing that hadn't been left plain. Unlike the outside of the temple/mound and the floor, it was carved in an intricated, mesmerizing swirling pattern so fine it must have taken hundreds of hours to complete.

"Now you need to prick your finger and smear blood on the death god's seal." Bishop frowned and ran his hands over the altar, sweeping away a thick layer of dust, revealing just how precise the swirling pattern was. "Here," he said, pointing to an intricate circular symbol in the center of all the intricate swirls. "Smear your blood here."

"Which finger?" Cyrus asked me, stepping up beside me, his claws extending from his fingers.

"How much blood do you need?" I asked Bishop, who was back to reading the piece of paper.

"It doesn't say. A good smear if you can manage it," he said with a shrug.

Which meant the wound was going to be deeper than a papercut, might need a bandage, and be a pain for a few days, but thankfully no worse than that.

"This one," I told Cyrus, holding out my left ring finger. It was a finger that I hopefully wouldn't use as much as my other ones for the next few days.

Cyrus nicked my fingertip, his claws so sharp I didn't feel it at first. Then my blood welled over my skin and I felt the sting. I smeared a large red streak across the symbol, squeezed my fingertip to draw out even more blood, and added another streak just to be sure while Cyrus nicked Knox's finger and he did the same.

"Place your palm on the seal and keep it there until the spell is done," Bishop commanded. "Whil's instructions say, don't worry if you touch the blood or each other. Knox, when I say go, I want you to pour Whil's potion over both of your hands and the blood." He uncorked the vial of golden liquid and handed it to Knox. "Then both of you repeat what I say. Got it?"

I placed my hand on the symbol and nodded that I understood, while Knox did the same, his fingers on top of mine, his hand almost big enough to cover the seal by himself.

A hint of desire shivered down my spine and pooled between my thighs, a reminder of the mating bond we were trying to break. Knox's eyes narrowed, and he sucked in a sharp breath as if he, too, could feel the urging from the bond.

Then the muscles in his jaw flexed, his eyes narrowed, and the icy hollowness of his rejection swelled, devouring the need and leaving me shivering not just from the cold in the chamber.

"Okay," Bishop said as he and Cyrus took a large step back.

Knox raised his gaze, finally meeting mine. His eyes were still a normal brown with no hint of his wolf, and for a second, I was falling inside their hard depths. They were so unlike Bishop's warm eyes and yet so very much the same, and I ached for him, for us, for what never should have been.

For just a second, hope and desperation flickered in those brown flecked with green depths, then he blinked, releasing me, and the hard mask he'd been wearing since I'd seen him in his human form returned.

"Ready?" he asked, his voice gruff, his body so tense a vein in his temple had started throbbing.

"Ready," I told him and he poured the potion out of the vial, trailing it over our hands and onto the seal and making sure some of it landed on the blood. A sudden jolt of power snapped through me and heat swept from my hand and up my arm, almost too hot in contrast to how cold I was.

"Oh, gree-ate god-ESS," Bishop said, his pronunciation strange as if he no longer knew exactly how to speak his own language.

"Oh, great goddess," I repeated.

"Oh, pow-erful ru-EL-er over the EEE-ternal slu-umber and the EEE-nd of all things," he continued. "I sta-and before you with hope-E, DEE-sire, and HU-mility. Heear my plea and gr-ANT your gree-atest mercies and might that I, your most HU-umble sea-er-vant, might sever and EE-x-cute the magic that Buh-hinds me. Oh, most REE-vered, awesome, and May-ges-tic ru-EL-er of death."

Knox and I repeated it all and waited...

And waited...

Time dragged forward with only the initial heat from Whil's magical liquid warming my hand and forearm.

My pulse pounded in my ears, and I held my breath, hoping and praying that it would work.

Knox deserved to be free. I hadn't meant to bond with him, hell, we didn't even know each other, he shouldn't have to be stuck with me for the rest of his life.

Please. If there was a death god asleep under my feet, please let her hear my prayer and free him. *Please.*

Sudden, ferocious light exploded from the shimmering golden liquid and the heat from the power turned into an inferno. It raced past my shoulder, into my chest, and flooded around my heart, stealing my breath, and painfully tearing into me, threatening to consume me. Every muscle in my body locked, the force of the power the only thing holding me up, and it jerked me upright, my head thrown back on a scream I couldn't release.

The pressure and agony was more powerful than anything I'd ever felt before. Even Cyrus's crushing power outside the temple that had brought me to my knees in an instant was nothing compared to the force ripping into my very essence.

But a mating bond was a powerful form of magic that no one had ever broken before. The magic needed to destroy something so strong had to be a force unlike any other, and I feared that force was going to tear me apart with the bond.

Don't miss the next book in the series!

Wolf Desired
Ensnared by the Pack: Book Three

My heat is back and there's no escaping it...

I was foolish to think I was back in control of my body, and now the heat I shouldn't have had in the first place has returned, burning into a dangerous fever that threatens my life.

I can't beat it alone. I need the guys.

Except our relationships are still uncertain and I don't know if I count on them? Knox is still furious at me for accidentally mate-bonding with him, Cyrus wants nothing to do with me, and while things with Bishop are good, our relationship is still new. And very fragile. Just like me.

This new realm is changing my body in unpredictable ways and I'm afraid I'm not strong enough to survive.

But I have to.

I *will*.

This is my chance at a new life, and I refuse to give up. I've already escaped a man-eating monster. I can escape a fate that says a powerless shifter is a worthless shifter.

OTHER BOOKS BY TESSA COLE

THE NEPHILIM'S DESTINY SERIES

Destined Shadows, prequel story

Destined Darkness, book 1

Destined Blood, book 2

Destined Fire, book 3

Destined Storm, book 4

Destined Radiance, book 5

THE ANGEL'S FATE SERIES

Fated Bonds, book 1

Fated Winter, book 2

Fated Fear, book 3

Fated Despair, book 4

Fated Resolve, book 5

Fated Heart, book 6

THE GRECIAN GODDESS TRILOGY

Kiss of the Goddess, book 1

Power of the Goddess, book 2

Bonds of the Goddess, book 3

ENSNARED BY THE PACK

www.ingramcontent.com/pod-product-compliance
Lightning Source LLC
Chambersburg PA
CBHW030121180626
46812CB00002B/505